Room for Light

Room for Magic
Book 2

Annika Stone

I

Room for Light

Chapter One

Kelsey Winters had photographed sunrise at the Starlight Arbor Inn exactly once before—October third, the morning she'd left, her camera capturing what her heart couldn't hold. Now, two months later, she stood in the same spot where she'd said goodbye, her breath crystallizing in the December air as she raised her camera again.

The inn looked so different dressed in winter white. Snow swept along the slate Victorian roof in soft curves. Icicles hung like crystal fringe from the wraparound porch and the eaves of that crazy turret on the left. Every window glowed amber against the pre-dawn purpled sky. Through her viewfinder, it looked like something from a snow globe—which made her think of the actual sand globe in the lobby, which made her think of magic, which made her think of Marcus Chen's weary bruised doctor's eyes the last time she'd seen him.

Click.

She photographed to avoid thinking, to turn four dimensions into two, to make the overwhelming manageable. It was easier to face the inn through her lens, where she could control the frame, the focus, the story being told. Where she couldn't smell the wood smoke curling from the chimneys or feel the way her heart stuttered at being back.

Click. Click.

The Lighthouse Keeper's Room—second floor, lake view, the window where Marcus had stood that last morning—was dark. Not that she was looking. Not that she'd angled her trusty Subaru specifically to see if warm light spilled from those particular curtains.

She'd been driving since three AM, fueled by truck stop coffee and the kind of restless energy that had kept her moving for the past two months. Copper Harbor, Marquette, a dozen small towns with stories to document and lighthouses to preserve in pixels. Always moving, because movement felt safer than stillness. Because staying anywhere too long meant risking what she'd felt here in October—that terrifying sensation of roots trying to grow.

Finally lowering her camera, Kelsey forced herself to move. The snow crunched under her boots with that particular squeak of powder over ice, each step a small percussion in the continual song of the lake winds. She could taste the cold—sharp and clean, carrying the mineral bite of Lake Michigan and something sweeter, like the ghost of wood smoke from chimneys she couldn't yet see.

Coming around the side of the inn to the main entry was like walking into a photograph she'd taken but never quite captured. The one that lived in her memory from October, now transformed by winter's heavy hand. Where autumn had painted the misty cream and white Victorian in warm golds and crimsons, winter had draped it in pristine white that made every architectural detail pop like calligraphy against fresh paper. The cream trim had become a study in contrasts—clean lines that drew her photographer's eye to the intricate gingerbread work under the eaves.

But it was the lake that stopped her cold.

Lake Michigan stretched endlessly gray-blue, darker than October's jeweled surface, with a cold intensity that made the horizon disappear into pewter sky. The dunes, starting a short stroll from the inn, rolled toward the water in gentle white curves, looking deceptively soft. She knew they'd be hard-packed beneath, sculpted by wind into patterns that begged to be photographed. The bare trees traced delicate black lines against the snow, their branches reaching like calligraphy strokes in the sky. She wanted to capture all of it. But it would never translate the way this moment felt—standing here again, breathing the lung-pinching air that tasted like memory and possibility.

Her fingers found her camera automatically, but for once she didn't raise it. This was too big, too encompassing to frame. This was the feeling she'd been chasing for two months. Every lighthouse, every coastal shot, every attempt to recreate the sense of belonging that had terrified her in October.

The scent reached her as she moved closer to the porch—wood smoke definitely, but underneath it, something that made her stomach tighten with recognition. Vanilla. Cinnamon. The particular smell of this place that seemed to live in her camera bag, her clothes, her hair for weeks after leaving. Not just the kitchen's baking, but something deeper. The scent of old wood that had absorbed generations of comfort, of wool rugs and lemon oil and whatever indefinable thing made a place feel like home instead of just shelter.

Her boots found the familiar rhythm of the porch steps, though now they were treacherous with a thin layer of ice under the snow. Five steps up—she remembered that from October, the way the third one creaked slightly, the way the fifth brought you level with the porch railing that was exactly the right height to lean against while watching sunrise over the lake.

The porch itself felt larger in winter, the white rocking chairs covered and pushed back against the house, making space for snow that had drifted in spiral patterns across the painted floor. Her breath caught as she noticed that someone—Agnes, probably—had swept a clear path to the door, but only that. The rest of the porch lay pristine, unmarked except for what looked like bird tracks leading from the railing to disappear under the nearest chair.

The double doors stood before her, painted forest green with brass hardware that had aged to a soft gold. She remembered these doors from October—solid oak with glass panels etched in a pattern that had looked like ivy then but now, backlit by the warm interior light, looked almost like stars. The doors were propped open just slightly, just enough to let a ribbon of golden light spill across the snow-dusted porch, just enough to let the scent of cinnamon rolls and coffee and whatever magic this place harbored drift out to welcome her.

She stood there for a moment, camera heavy around her neck, luggage handles cutting into her gloved fingers, breathing in winter air that tasted like memory and exhaling something that felt dangerously close to hope. In October, she'd documented everything. This time, she wanted to feel it first, capture it second.

The doors opened wider, spilling more golden light across the snow-covered porch. Kelsey lowered her camera, expecting Ella Thompson or maybe Mrs. Frankl starting their early morning routines. Instead, Agnes Kowalski emerged, wrapped in a thick cardigan that did nothing to soften her angular frame. Even at this impossible hour, her steel-gray hair was pinned into a perfect chignon, and her pale eyes held the sharp focus of someone who'd been managing details since before dawn.

"You planning to freeze out there all morning, or are you coming in?"

The older woman's voice carried clearly across the still air, stern and welcoming at once. Kelsey fumbled her lens cap, nearly dropping it in the snow. She hadn't planned to check in this early—hadn't planned much beyond arriving and figuring out the rest later.

"I didn't think anyone would be up yet," she called back, hefting her camera bag and starting toward the door.

"Inn's always awake for arrivals." Agnes held the door wider. "Especially expected ones."

Kelsey paused at the bottom of the porch steps. "I don't have a reservation. I just thought—"

"The Dune Walker's Room waits for you." Agnes said it matter-of-factly, as if rooms could wait, as if the inn itself had been holding space. "Been ready since Friday. Beatrice had a feeling you'd be early."

Friday. Three days ago. Before Kelsey herself had

decided to cut short her Pictured Rocks assignment and drive through the night. A chill that had nothing to do with December ran down her spine.

Stepping across the threshold was like being embraced by memory made tangible. The soaring lobby enveloped her in warmth that went beyond temperature—warm misty green walls, dark oak floor bright with polish, that crazy teardrop chandelier that made the wide, curving staircase glow. The air thick with story, with vanilla and cinnamon drifting from the distant kitchen, and just a hint of wood smoke, probably from the parlor fireplace. Underneath it all, that indefinable scent of old houses that had sheltered love and laughter and countless homecomings.

The big clear glass sand globe commanded the space from its square mahogany pedestal. The sand was quiet now, but it could swirl and dance in a way that defied photography. Brass wall lamps caught the blond light from the chandelier.

"Coffee?" Agnes asked, already moving behind the sweeping, tall front desk with surprising efficiency. "You look like you could use it. The real stuff, not that truck-stop swill."

"How did you—" Kelsey stopped herself. Two months ago, she'd documented impossible things in this place. A little omniscience about her caffeine consumption hardly registered on the scale of magical oddities.

Agnes's mouth twitched in what might have been a smile. "You're a photographer driving since before dawn in December. Doesn't take magic to figure that out." She pushed the old-fashioned registration book across the polished wood. "Sign here. Same rate as October."

As Kelsey signed her name, she noticed the book was already open to today's date, her name penciled lightly in the margin as if someone had been practicing writing it. Or as if the inn itself had been preparing.

"Is Mrs. Frankl—?"

"Coming in at seven. She's busy training Ella on the wedding tea ceremonies this week." Agnes collected a familiar brass key from somewhere under the desk. "The Chen boy isn't here yet, if you're wondering."

The name hit Kelsey like a bolt of electricity. Her pulse jumped, heat flooded up her neck, her hand clenched involuntarily around the pen. She could feel Agnes watching her reaction and tried to school her features, but her body had already betrayed her. Two months of careful distance undone by two syllables.

"I wasn't—"

"Course not." Agnes's tone was perfectly neutral, which somehow made it worse. "He'll be here Thursday, weather permitting. Something about shifts at the hospital."

Thursday. The word lodged under her ribs like a splinter. Kelsey focused on adjusting her camera bag's strap, avoiding Agnes's knowing gaze. She'd been very careful not to ask about Marcus Chen. The fact that Agnes answered anyway felt like the inn's first move in a game Kelsey wasn't sure she wanted to play.

"Here." Agnes came around the desk, reaching for one of Kelsey's equipment bags with surprising strength. "Can't have you hauling this monster up the stairs alone. Your hands are shaking from the cold."

They weren't shaking from the cold, but Kelsey let Agnes take the bag anyway. The older woman led the way up the familiar staircase, her tread soft on the deep blue carpet runner. Kelsey's fingers trailed along the banister, satiny smooth, the wood worn by countless hands over more than a century. The stairs themselves were solid oak, each step creating its own note—the third one with its distinctive creak, the seventh that sang slightly under pressure, creating a quiet symphony as they climbed.

The walls along the stairway were gallery-perfect, lined with black and white photographs of the inn through the decades. She'd studied them in October—guests on the porch in 1920s clothes, the inn draped in bunting for some long-ago celebration, a wedding party from the 1960s with the bride in a dress that barely reached her thighs. Now, in the early morning light filtering through tall windows, the photographs seemed to watch her climb, as if the inn's history was taking her measure.

The second floor hallway stretched before them, wide enough for the inn's grand aspirations but intimate enough to feel welcoming. The runner beneath their feet was the same blue as the stairs, muffling their footsteps but not quite hiding the gentle protests of old floorboards. Brass sconces lined the walls, their warm light creating pools of gold against cream-colored wallpaper that featured the faintest pattern of climbing roses. Door after door lined the hallway—some with brass nameplates that caught the light, others with numbers in the same elegant script she remembered from October.

"Wedding preparations are coming along," Agnes said. "Though between you and me, that sand globe's been acting up something fierce. Showing all sorts of things nobody asked to see."

"What kinds of things?"

Agnes paused at the second-floor landing, giving Kelsey a look that seemed to see straight through her defensive armor. The landing was a small haven unto itself—a circular space with a tall window that faced the lake, a velvet-cushioned window seat that invited lingering, a small table holding fresh flowers that shouldn't exist in December but somehow did. The morning light streaming through created patterns on the opposite wall, and Kelsey could smell the faint scent of the flowers—something like freesia mixed with winter air.

"Future things. Past things. Things that might be, if people are brave enough."

Before Kelsey could formulate a response that didn't sound like panic, Agnes was moving again, leading her down the hallway. They passed doors Kelsey remembered—the Rose Suite where honeymooners stayed, the Harbor Master's Room with its nautical theme, the Lighthouse Keeper's Room where Marcus had—

She stopped herself from looking too closely at that particular door, though she couldn't help noticing it was slightly ajar, revealing only darkness within. No warm light, no sign of occupancy. Of course not. Thursday, Agnes had said. Weather permitting.

The Dune Walker's Room stood directly across the way, its brass nameplate gleaming in the sconce light. Kelsey remembered thinking in October that the name suited her—always walking, always moving, never staying long enough to sink into sand. Now the irony felt sharper. She was back, after all. The walker had returned to walk the same dunes, the same halls, the same dangerous territory of maybe-belonging.

The door opened at Agnes's touch—no key needed. Stepping inside was like being welcomed by an old friend who'd been patiently waiting.

The Dune Walker's Room breathed around her,

morning light streaming through tall windows that faced the dunes and the lake. The walls were painted the color of driftwood, a soft gray-brown that shifted in interesting ways with the light. The hardwood floors gleamed honey-gold beneath her feet. The scent hit her immediately—lavender and lake air, the faint mustiness of old quilts, and something else, something that belonged specifically to this room. In October, she'd decided it smelled like possibility.

Now it smelled like coming home.

The room was exactly as she'd left it, but also impossibly different. The four-poster bed still dominated the space, its white linens crisp and welcoming, the wedding ring quilt folded precisely at the foot. The writing desk still sat in the alcove created by the smaller window, positioned perfectly for watching the lake's moods. The dark green overstuffed chair by the radiator still invited long conversations with herself and the view.

But her photographs from October hung on the walls—the ones she'd taken of the inn, of the town, of the lighthouse at sunset. She'd shared them with Ella as part of their emailed conversations last month, during which Ella had somehow convinced her to shoot Ella's wedding this weekend.

The photos were framed in unpolished pine, arranged with an eye for composition that suggested someone who understood photography, who'd seen what she'd been trying to capture in each shot.

Her breath caught as she moved closer to examine them. There was the inn at golden hour, the Victorian details sharp against the autumn sky. The lighthouse standing sentinel against Lake Michigan's endless blue. The dunes rolling away like sleeping giants. Or lynxes, according to local legend. Agnes washing windows with fierce concentration. Mrs. Frankl arranging flowers, her face soft with the pleasure of someone creating beauty.

And there, in a small frame near the window—Marcus. She'd captured him without him knowing, standing on the inn's porch with coffee steaming in his hands, looking out at the lake with an expression of such longing it had made her chest ache even then. She'd titled it in her head "Homesick," though she'd never been sure if he was homesick for this place or somewhere else entirely.

"How—?"

"The inn appreciates being seen," Agnes said simply, setting down the equipment bag. "Especially by someone who sees it true."

On the pillow sat a book Kelsey didn't remember leaving behind. She moved closer, her eye catching the worn leather binding, the gilt letters faded with age: Lighthouses of the Great Lakes: A Guardian's Guide.

Inside the front cover, in handwriting that looked old-fashioned but somehow familiar:

To K

Some lights are worth waiting for

M

Her hands trembled as she traced the inscription. It couldn't be from Marcus. The book was clearly vintage, probably from the 1960s based on the binding style. Which meant...

"Inn's been busy, I see," Agnes observed, not sounding particularly surprised. "It does that sometimes. Finds things that need finding."

"But this is impossible."

Agnes headed for the door, pausing at the threshold. "Breakfast runs until nine, but Beatrice usually saves the best pastries for family." She paused. "Welcome back, dear."

The door closed with a soft click, leaving Kelsey alone with her impossible photographs, an impossible book, and the impossible sensation of the inn wrapping around her like a warm quilt. As if it had been waiting.

Chapter Two

Kelsey set the lighthouse book carefully on the round marble nightstand and moved to the bigger window. The lighthouse stood in the distance, dark against the lightening sky. In October, it had blazed to life at the worst possible moment—or the best, depending on how honest she was being with herself. Now it waited, patient as winter, for whatever came next.

Her phone buzzed. A text from her mother: *Got there safe?*

Kelsey typed back: *Yes. All roads clear*

She didn't mention the three AM departure or the way her hands had gripped the steering wheel tighter the closer she got to Green Arbor. Didn't mention that she'd told herself she was coming early to help with wedding preparations, to photograph the inn in winter light, to document the town's Christmas festivities. All true. None of them the truth.

The truth was simpler and more terrifying: she'd missed this place. Missed the way morning light fell through these windows. Missed Agnes and her sisters' happy bickering and Mrs. Frankl's knowing looks. Missed the sense of belonging she'd never let herself feel anywhere else.

Missed Marcus Chen, with his neat collar and sleep-worn eyes and the way he'd kissed her like she was something special.

Thursday, Agnes had said. Weather permitting.

She hung her puffy coat in the stand-up wardrobe that smelled faintly of lavender and lake air, and set her gloves and hat on the inner shelf. She could sneak out the kitchen door and grab her luggage after a bit. Wouldn't need the coat for that, with the tank top, mock turtleneck, and thick wool sweater she still had on. Two of her cameras went on the dresser, arranged just so. Laptop on the small writing desk where she'd edited photos late into October nights, trying to capture magic in pixels.

The lighthouse book watched from the nightstand like a patient reminder.

By the time she'd arranged everything exactly right—her typical ritual for making any space temporarily hers—the sun had fully risen, setting the snow outside ablaze with morning light. Her stomach growled, reminding her that truck stop coffee wasn't actually a food group.

She made her way downstairs, a camera slung around her out of habit more than intention. The inn was waking up around her—the loud then soft clatter of breakfast preparations as the kitchen door swung open and closed. The sound of doors opening and closing, and a voice carrying from the dining room. The sand globe swirled as she passed, forming what looked like two figures in the snow, but she didn't let herself look too closely.

The dining room was nearly empty—probably typical for a Monday in mid-December. But stepping into the space still took Kelsey's breath away, the way it had in October when she'd first glimpsed it through the French doors.

The room belonged to a more gracious era, when breakfast was ceremony rather than fuel. Tall windows marched along the lake-facing wall, their panes divided into small squares that caught and fractured the winter light into geometric patterns across the hardwood floors. The walls were painted the same soft cream as the hall-ways, but here they were adorned with botanical prints in matching frames—detailed illustrations of Michigan wildflowers and trees that someone had clearly chosen with care.

A massive mahogany sideboard dominated one wall, its surface gleaming with the kind of polish that spoke of daily attention. Above it, an oil painting of the inn in its early days showed the building surrounded by virgin forest, no dunes visible yet, Lake Michigan a distant blue promise through the trees. The artist had captured something eternal about the place—the sense that it had always been here, would always be here, patient as stone.

Tables were scattered throughout the space with apparent casualness, but Kelsey's photographer's eye caught the careful composition—each positioned to take advantage of the light, to create intimate conversation pockets while maintaining the room's sense of openness. The tables themselves were works of art, dark wood that matched the sideboard, each set with blue willow china that looked old enough to be original to the inn. Real cloth napkins in deep blue sat beside each place setting, and small crystal glasses caught the window light like scattered jewels.

The scent in here was different from the lobby's vanilla and wood smoke—more immediate, domestic. Fresh coffee, obviously, but underneath that traces of maple syrup, the yeast-sweet smell of bread baking somewhere nearby, and was that nutmeg?

But it was the Christmas lights that transformed the space from merely elegant to magical. Tiny white lights had been strung around every window frame, their warm glow competing with the winter daylight. They reflected in the china, the crystal, the polished wood, creating a galaxy of little stars that made the whole room feel like the inside of a jewelry box. The effect should have been overwhelming, but instead it felt festive, welcoming, like the inn was putting on its best dress for the holidays.

Only three other tables were occupied—an older couple sharing the newspaper over what looked like their regular morning routine, a woman in a business pantsuit typing on her laptop while her eggs grew cold, and a man in his fifties reading a paperback thriller while steadily working through a stack of pancakes that defied physics. Each seemed content in their solitude, but Kelsey noticed they all looked up and smiled when Beatrice passed, the kind of acknowledgment that spoke of familiarity, of being known.

Kelsey chose a corner table with her back to the wall and a view of both the entrance and the windows overlooking the lake. Old habits from a childhood of constantly moving: always know your exits, always see who's coming.

Beatrice appeared at her elbow, her round figure moving with surprising speed as she carried a pot of coffee. Where Agnes was all sharp angles and efficiency, her younger sister was soft curves and warmth—flour still dusting her floral apron, silver-blonde curls escaping from a loose bun, smile bright enough to power the Christmas lights strung along the windows.

"Kelsey! Oh, Agnes said you were back but I hardly believed—look at you, thin as a rail! Have you been eating at all?" Without waiting for an answer, she was pouring coffee into a sturdy white mug. "I'll bring you the works. Pancakes, eggs, that apple butter you liked. Can't have you wasting away."

"I'm fine, really—"

"Nonsense. You're family." Beatrice squeezed her shoulder with surprising strength. "Besides, we need you strong for the wedding preparations. So much to do!"

She bustled away before Kelsey could protest that she wasn't actually family, that she was just here to help document the wedding, that she didn't need special treatment. The coffee was perfect—strong and hot with just a hint of cinnamon, though she hadn't mentioned how she took it.

Through the windows, snow had begun falling, easy, fat flakes that made the world look soft.

The lighthouse stood dark in the distance, waiting.

Looking at it, she couldn't help remembering another October night when she'd stared at that same lighthouse from the Dune Climb parking lot. Liam had driven them—her and Marcus—to the National Lakeshore for the astronomical society's star party. She'd brought her camera for long-exposure shots of the Milky Way, told herself it was just for the portfolio opportunity.

But then Marcus had stood beside her in the darkness, close enough that she could smell his cologne—clean and woody that made her think of cedar closets and safety. The astronomer had been pointing out constellations, but all Kelsey could focus on was the way Marcus's breath caught when she accidentally brushed his hand reaching for her lens cap.

"Can you see Cassiopeia?" he'd asked. She'd made some noise of agreement, though she'd been looking at the way starlight caught in his eyes instead of searching the sky.

Liam had been there too, somewhere, but he might as well have been on the moon. Her whole world had narrowed to the warm presence beside her, to the way Marcus stepped closer when the lake breeze picked up, how his hand found the small of her back to steady her on the uneven sand.

"Cold?" he'd murmured, and she'd shaken her head even though she was shivering. Not from cold. From the electric awareness of him, from wanting to lean back into his warmth, from the terrifying realization that she was falling for someone she'd known for not even three days.

That was the night before the lighthouse incident. Before that kiss. Before she'd run.

Her phone sat silent on the table. No messages. Not that she expected any. She and Marcus had texted a few times after October—careful, friendly messages about work and weather and nothing that mattered. The kind of conversations people had when they were trying not to have the conversation that counted.

Beatrice returned with enough food to feed three people, fussing over the placement of the plates and the temperature of the syrup. The apple butter was exactly as Kelsey remembered—Sarah's secret recipe that Agnes guarded like a dragon with its hoard.

"Cordelia says the lighthouse has been acting up," Beatrice said, refilling coffee Kelsey had barely touched.

Kelsey's fork paused halfway to her mouth. "Acting up how?"

"Oh, you know. Lighthouse things." Beatrice waved a hand vaguely. "Turning on at odd hours. Harold Weatherby swears he saw it blazing at three in the morning last week, but you know Harold. Marcus Chen called about it, actually. Wanted to make sure someone had checked the electrical."

The fork clattered against her plate. Kelsey winced at the noise. "Marcus called about the lighthouse?"

"Tuesday, I think it was." Beatrice tapped her chin. "Maybe Monday? Said something about making sure it was safe before—" Beatrice's eyes widened as if she'd said too much. "Well. Anyway. You eat up, you hear?"

She slid away, toward the older couple's table, before Kelsey could form a coherent question.

Tuesday. The same day the inn had apparently started preparing her room. The same day she'd cut short her assignment and started driving south.

Through the window, the lighthouse remained steadfastly dark. But Kelsey could swear she felt it watching her, waiting for something. Just like the book upstairs with its impossible inscription. Just like the inn itself, humming with barely contained anticipation.

The coffee mug warmed her hands—steady hands now, photographer's hands that knew how to hold still even when everything inside was shaking. Three days to decide if she was brave enough to stop running. Three days before Thursday, weather permitting.

Her phone buzzed against the table, the sound too loud in the quiet dining room. Not a text this time—a voicemail notification. From a Chicago number she knew by heart.

Her finger hovered over the play button. Around her, the inn seemed to hold its breath. Even the sand globe's endless swirling slowed.

She pressed play, held the phone to her ear.

"Kelsey." Marcus's voice, rougher than she remembered, like he'd just come off a long shift. "I know we haven't... I mean, I heard you might be coming to the wedding. From Ella. She mentioned you were doing the photography."

A pause. She could hear hospital sounds in the background—pages, distant voices, the particular chaos of an emergency department.

"I'm driving up Thursday. I was wondering if you'd... if you wanted to talk. About—" Another pause, longer this time. "About the lighthouse. I keep thinking about the lighthouse. Anyway. I'll be there Thursday. Weather permitting."

The message ended. Kelsey set the phone down carefully, as if it might explode.

Weather permitting. The same phrase Agnes had used. Like the whole universe was conspiring, making sure she knew exactly when her carefully maintained distance would collapse.

She looked out at the lighthouse again, quiet against the winter sky, and remembered the weight of his hand on her back. The way he'd said her name like it mattered. The way he'd kissed her like she was worth staying awake for after a thirty-six-hour shift.

Outside, the snow continued to fall, transforming Green Arbor into the kind of winter postcard that made people believe in magic. And upstairs in the Dune Walker's Room, a lighthouse keeper's guide waited on a nightstand, its inscription promising that some lights were worth waiting for.

Even if you'd spent your whole life learning to leave before the waiting could hurt you.

Even then.

Especially then.

Chapter Three

Doctor Marcus Chen had been awake for thirty-six hours when he passed the exit for Grand Rapids on Route 131, and the smart thing would have been to stop. Find a hotel. Sleep for twelve hours. Show up at his aunt's inn rested and ready to pretend everything was fine.

Instead, he pressed harder on the accelerator, chasing his headlights through increasingly heavy snow.

His hands ached from gripping the wheel, knuckles white despite his best efforts to relax. His eyes burned with the grit of too many hours under fluorescent lights, and his mouth tasted like the metallic aftermath of hospital coffee and the granola bar he'd forced down six hours ago. Maybe seven. Time had gone fluid somewhere around hour twenty-eight.

The radio muttered about winter storm warnings, but Marcus had grown up in midwest winters. He knew how to read the way snow slanted across highway lights, how to feel when pavement shifted from wet to icy through the steering wheel's subtle shimmies. His hands remained steady—emergency physician hands that could intubate a patient while the trauma bay exploded in chaos around him.

Steady hands that hadn't been quite steady enough six hours ago.

Juliette Garcia. Thirty-four. Mother of two.

He cranked the heat higher, but the chill in his chest remained. Under his winter coat, he still wore his hospital scrubs, the navy ones that made him look competent and professional and like someone who could save lives. They clung to him now, stiff with old sweat, carrying the smell of antiseptic and the sharp, bitter scents of the ER—fear and floor cleaner and the iron tang of blood. The silk shirt he'd worn for rounds —his armor—lay crumpled in his locker back in Chicago, abandoned after the third hour of the trauma that wouldn't stabilize.

His phone, mounted on the dashboard, lit up with another text from his mother. The screen's brightness stabbed at his exhausted eyes, making him squint. He didn't need to have the care read it to him to know what it said. Some variation of "These things happen" or

"You can't save everyone" or "The statistics were against her from the moment of impact." Somewhere in the fourth or fifth hour, he'd called to consult with her. Still tied to those apron strings. Dr. Helena Chen had a surgeon's ability to compartmentalize, to reduce human tragedy to medical probability.

Marcus had inherited her hands but not her distance.

The heater was making his head swim, that disconnected feeling when exhaustion met warmth. He cracked the window, letting in a slice of winter air that bit at his face and carried the clean smell of snow. Better. The cold kept him sharp, kept him from drifting into the micro-sleeps that had been threatening since Big Rapids.

His neck ached from tension, shoulders bunched up around his ears. Every muscle felt like it had been clenched for the entire four-hour drive and counting.

Traverse City emerged through the snow. Last chance for a hotel, for sleep, for showing up at the Starlight Arbor Inn like a functional human being instead of whatever he was right now.

Then he saw it: a brown highway sign with a lighthouse symbol. "Scenic Route to Roaming Lynx Dunes."

The lighthouse.

His chest tightened with something that wasn't exhaustion. He rolled on through.

I keep thinking about the lighthouse

His own voice on Kelsey's voicemail three days ago, when he'd stood in the break room between traumas and let himself say what he'd been thinking for two months. The break room had smelled like reheated fish —someone's sad dinner—and his voice had echoed off the walls. Not "I miss you" or "I can't stop thinking about that kiss" or "I've been saving your texts like breadcrumbs leading somewhere I'm afraid to go."

Just: *I keep thinking about the lighthouse*

As if she'd understand that he meant the moment when it blazed to life, when her mouth had been soft under his and tasted like surprise and belonging. When he'd understood with perfect, terrifying clarity that he could fall in love with this woman who documented everything except her own heart.

He could still feel the way she'd trembled against him, just slightly, like a bird deciding whether to fly or stay. Could still smell her shampoo—something citrus and green, lime and basil maybe. The way she'd pulled back after, eyes wide, and whispered "Oh," like she'd discovered something terrifying and wonderful at once. Her fingers had been cold when they'd touched his face, just briefly, before she'd reached for her camera. Her armor.

Traverse City passed in a blur of snow and streetlights that hurt to look at directly. His rental car—because of course his practical Accord had chosen this week to need transmission work—handled differently than he was used to. The steering wheel was too thick, the heater vents in the wrong places, everything slightly off, like the world had shifted two degrees while he wasn't paying attention. The new car smell mixed unpleasantly with the hospital scents still clinging to him.

He told the car to play his mother's text: *Heard about the spinal case. These things happen. You did everything right.*

Everything right except save her.

He thought about calling his dad. James Chen would be awake, grading music theory papers or working on a composition. He'd listen without judgment, maybe play something gentle over the phone—Chopin or Debussy, the kind of music that made Marcus remember beauty existed even amid multiple traumas.

But calling his father meant admitting he was driving through a snowstorm on no sleep toward a woman who might not want him there. It meant voicing the fear that he was becoming his mother—brilliant at his job, terrible at everything else.

The sign for Green Arbor appeared through the snow like a promise: "Population 261. Where Magic Meets the Lake."

Marcus had laughed at that tagline in October. Now, exhausted and raw and running on hospital coffee fumes and muscle memory, he wasn't laughing.

He'd seen the inn's magic firsthand, felt it in the way rooms seemed to know what guests needed. Had kissed Kelsey Winters while the lighthouse—defunct for twenty years—suddenly blazed like a beacon calling ships home.

He felt the memory in his body. The way she'd tasted like the coffee they'd shared that morning mixed with something sweet. The little sound she'd made when his hand found the small of her back. How afterward, she'd pressed her fingers to her lips like she was trying to hold the kiss there, then immediately reached for her camera.

The snow had eased to fat, lazy flakes that danced in his headlights. The last five miles took forever and no time at all. One moment he was on M-22, between empty fields that smelled like winter and farmland, the next he was turning onto Main Street. Christmas lights twinkled in every window, turning the falling snow red and green and gold. The hardware store where Liam's family had probably sold nails and knowledge for generations. The take-out place that had fifty kinds of hot dog toppings, none of which had appealed to a picky, pretty photographer. She'd had mint chocolate chip ice cream instead. In October, while her nose turned pink from cold.

Then, finally, impossibly: the Starlight Arbor Inn.

The Victorian sprawled before him like something from a dream, all cream paint and gingerbread trim made softer by snow. The lobby lights glowed dim but warm behind frosted windows, and a lamp flickered in what he knew was the kitchen. One window on the second floor—the Dune Walker's Room—showed the restless light of someone awake at an ungodly hour. Otherwise, the inn slept, peaceful under its blanket of snow.

The parking lot held four cars covered in white: two practical SUVs, a truck with a snowplow attachment, and a Subaru with Colorado plates still visible through the snow. His chest constricted.

Kelsey.

His hands—so steady on the highway—trembled as he shifted into park. His pulse jumped, skin suddenly too warm despite the cold.

He'd known she'd be here. Had been both dreading and needing this moment for three days, ever since Ella mentioned she'd hired Kelsey to photograph the wedding. But knowing and seeing were different things, and the evidence of her presence—that familiar Subaru with the small dent in the bumper—punched the air from his lungs.

He could almost see her hands on that steering wheel, the way she gripped things when nervous—white-knuckled but trying to look casual. Could picture her checking her mirrors obsessively, the way she'd done during their one shared car ride to the lighthouse tour, when he'd wanted to reach over and smooth the worry line between her eyebrows but had kept his hands carefully to himself.

She was here. Three days early.

The engine ticked as it cooled, snow already beginning to veil his windshield. Somewhere behind those walls, Kelsey Winters was breathing. Existing.

Here.

Chapter Four

Marcus sat in the rapidly cooling rental car for three more minutes, watching snow accumulate on Kelsey's Subaru like time made visible. The Starlight Arbor Inn glowed before him, all those windows promising warmth, but he couldn't quite make himself move. Not yet.

Thirty-eight hours without sleep had made everything feel distant and too immediate at once. The parking lot could have been a thousand miles wide. His scrubs were sticking to his back, and he could smell himself—thirty-eight hours of hospital and highway and anxiety and blood.

But underneath all of that, something else. Hope, maybe. Or terror. At this level of exhaustion, they felt the same.

He grabbed his duffel from the back seat, packed in a hurry when he'd been called in early to work. Guardian might've been crammed in at the last minute. He'd seen the stuffed lynx in his closet and thought of October, of her laugh when he'd admitted to keeping childhood comfort objects. Not her polite laugh or her nervous laugh, but a real one—surprised and delighted and a little breathless, like joy had caught her off guard.

The parking lot was treacherous with new snow over ice. His dress shoes—stupid to drive in dress shoes, but he'd left straight from the hospital—slipped and slid. The cold cut through his unbuttoned coat and scrubs, making him gasp. Snow found its way into his collar immediately, melting against overheated skin.

The walk to the front door felt endless. Snow crunched under his inadequate shoes, and by the time he reached the covered porch, he was shivering hard enough to make his teeth click.

It was locked, of course. Past midnight on a Wednesday. Thursday, now. He found the after-hours bell, its brass button worn smooth by decades of late arrivals, and pressed it, then stood stomping snow from his shoes while he waited. The porch smelled like the evergreen garland strung along the railing and wound around its pillars.

Footsteps approached from inside, measured and unhurried. The lock turned with a well-oiled click, and

Aunt Mei-Lin appeared in her evening kimono, the burgundy one with embroidered cranes that she'd owned since before Marcus was born. She must've stayed over, waiting up for him just in case.

She studied his face, her dark eyes cataloging everything—the hollows under his eyes, the elastic band from the saline pouches he'd forgotten to take off, the way he swayed slightly on his feet. "Thirty-six hours awake?"

"Thirty-eight." The words came out rough, his throat raw from cold. He stepped into the warmth that smelled like home—wood polish and cinnamon and that special scent that meant safety. The heat slammed into him like a wall, making him dizzy.

"Too long." She locked the door behind him, her expression holding that mix of love and concern that had always made him feel twelve years old. "Kitchen."

He knew better than to argue. Mei-Lin Chen Frankl had her own way of healing, and it usually started with tea and truth in equal measure. She led him through the quiet lobby, past the hurricane lamp casting flickering shadows on cream walls, past the sand globe, quiet in the dark. Past the parlor where white ribbons and evergreen boughs suggested wedding preparations had begun, their pine scent sharp in the warm air.

The kitchen was same as ever, a big warm hug. Same scarred wooden table in the corner where he'd spent hours drawing superheroes saving the say during summer visits. Same ancient stove that had moods like a living thing, currently purring contentment. The room smelled like rising bread dough and the lingering ghosts of a thousand meals—onions and vanilla and well-used cast iron.

Marcus collapsed into his old chair, the one with the wobbly leg that you had to know how to balance. His aunt said nothing while she worked, letting the familiar sounds fill the space—water rushing into the kettle, the soft rustle of tea leaves, the click of the gas burner coming to life. The ritual of it soothed something raw in his chest.

The overhead light was too bright for his exhausted eyes, but the warmth seeping into his bones made up for it. He could feel himself starting to shut down, that dangerous edge where exhaustion became collapse.

"She's here," Mei-Lin said finally, setting a cup before him. The china clinked softly against the wooden table. The scent rose up—the "coming home" blend. Chamomile and lavender and something else, something that always made him think of happy summer afternoons.

But the words hit him like adrenaline straight to the heart—pulse spiking, hands suddenly unsteady around the delicate saucer. He had to set it down before he spilled tea everywhere, before his aunt saw how badly those two words affected him. The china rattled against wood, betraying him.

"I know," he said.

"Three days early."

"I know." His voice came out tougher than intended, like he'd been running. Or drowning.

"Your mother called. About the case."

He spread his hands on the worn wood of the table. Long, thin, clever fingers. "These things happen, right?"

"Your mother saves lives," his aunt said, settling across from him with her own cup. "You save lives. Noble work, both of you." She paused, letting the weight gather. "But who saves you, little one?"

The childhood nickname in Mandarin brought tears he had to blink away. The kitchen blurred for a moment. Exhaustion, just exhaustion.

The question hit like an accusation wrapped in love. Marcus stared blindly into his tea, seeing Juliette Garcia's terrified eyes in the amber liquid. Seeing his mother's surgical precision. Seeing his father's gentle hurt every time Helena missed another concert, another anniversary, another chance to choose family over calling. The tea smelled like peace, but all he could taste was failure.

"I'm good at my job," he said quietly.

"Yes. Your mother trained you well." Mei-Lin's voice held edges sharp as scalpels. "She chose the knife. I chose the cup. Both of us heal, Marcus. The difference is, I let people heal me back."

"Auntie Mei-Lin—"

"Your father never felt lesser," she interrupted, reading his mind the way she always had. "James knew his worth. Your mother just couldn't see that teaching children music, making beauty in the world—that's its own kind of saving."

Marcus thought of his father's hands on piano keys, coaxing melody from silence. Thought of his mother's hands in chest cavities, coaxing life from death. Thought of his own hands, steady in trauma but shaking now, useless.

Thought of Kelsey's hands, always in motion, documenting everything but never still enough to be documented.

"The girl doesn't sleep either," Mei-Lin observed, refilling his cup. "I hear her walking at all hours. That camera clicking like a nervous heartbeat."

Heat flooded his face like he was seventeen instead of thirty-five. His aunt's kimono rustled as she moved, and he caught a hint of her perfume—jasmine and something woody. "She's always been—"

"She photographs everything except what matters." His aunt's gaze was steady, knowing. "Reminds me of someone else who documents lives instead of living them."

The journal. Marcus's chest tightened. His aunt knew about the journal where he recorded every successful code, every life pulled back from the edge. His tally against the ones he couldn't save. The pages filled with times and medications and outcomes, as if writing them down could change the statistics.

Just like Kelsey with her photographs, building walls of images between herself and the world. He remembered catching her once without her camera, the way she'd looked lost and younger and almost scared until she could grab it again. The way her shoulders had relaxed once she had her armor back.

"I should get some sleep," he said, standing. The chair scraped against linoleum, too loud in the sleeping kitchen. Running. Always running, just like—

"Room's ready," Mei-Lin said simply. "Same one as October. I had a feeling you'd want familiar."

She pressed the brass key into his palm. It was warm from her hand, worn smooth by decades of use. He could feel the weight of it—not just metal but memory.

The walk to the second floor felt both endless and too quick. His feet found the quiet spots on the stairs from muscle memory, avoiding the creaky third and seventh steps. The carpet was soft under his wet shoes, muffling his steps but not the racing of his heart.

The hallway stretched before him, dark except for small nightlights shaped like stars—new since October

—casting gentle shadows on cream walls. The air up here smelled different, older, like lavender sachets and furniture polish and the ghost of a thousand dreams.

He paused outside the Dune Walker's Room. Light crept from beneath the door, and he could hear movement inside—soft footsteps pacing, the whisper of fabric, a pause by the window. His hand almost raised to knock before sanity reasserted itself.

Bad idea to start this now, exhausted and smelling like failure.

The Lighthouse Keeper's Room opened silently, the door swinging inward to reveal a space that looked exactly as he'd left it in October. As if it had been waiting. The same nautical prints on the walls, the same brass compass weather-thing by the window. The same view of the lighthouse through windows that rattled slightly in the wind.

But now winter had transformed the view. Where October had been gold and crimson, December was silver and white, the lighthouse standing dark against a star-bright sky. His room smelled like cedar and clean linen and something uniquely this room—maybe the wood polish they used on the ship's wheel mounted on the wall, maybe just the accumulated comfort of a space meant for rest.

He set his duffel on the bed and unzipped it, his fingers clumsy. His clothes smelled like his apartment, like the life he'd temporarily fled. And there, on top of his hastily packed clothes, was Guardian. The stuffed lynx looked back at him with button eyes, worn fabric soft under his touch, one ear permanently bent from being carried everywhere during a sometimes-difficult childhood.

He'd grabbed it at the last minute, standing in his Chicago apartment, knowing he should leave immediately. Had seen it on the closet shelf and thought of October, of admitting to Kelsey that he still had it, of her laugh—not mocking but understanding.

"Everyone needs something to hold onto," she'd said, showing him her camera strap worn thin from years of gripping. Then, quieter, like she was admitting something dangerous: "Mine just happens to take pictures."

The way she'd looked at him then, like maybe she wanted to hold onto something else, something more solid than worn leather and precision glass. But then Agnes had called them for tea, and the moment had broken.

Now he sat on the bed—the mattress creaking softly, dipping under his weight—holding Guardian like the ridiculous thirty-five-year-old man he was. Carrying childhood comfort into an adult situation he didn't know how to navigate. The lynx smelled like his apartment, like coffee and aftershave and the particular loneliness of coming home after overnight shifts.

Through the window, the lighthouse stood dark against the star-bright sky. Snow was falling harder again, and he could hear the wind picking up, rattling the sturdy old panes. He should shower, wash off the hospital smell, the highway grit, the weight of lives he couldn't save. His skin felt grimy, too tight, like it belonged to someone else.

Instead, he found himself pulling out his phone, thumb hovering over Kelsey's name in his contacts. The screen's brightness hurt his eyes in the dim room.

Three days since he'd left that voicemail.

Three days of silence that said everything.

He started typing. *I'm here. Can we talk?*

Deleted it.

The lighthouse is dark again tonight

Deleted it.

I brought Guardian. Remember when we laughed about him?

Stared at the words until his eyes burned. She'd probably think he was crazy, texting at midnight about a stuffed animal. His thumb moved to delete this one too, but his weariness made him clumsy. He hit send instead.

The message hung there, delivered, irretrievable.

"Shit," he muttered, then louder: "Shit."

Three dots appeared immediately. She was awake.

She was typing. His heart hammered against his ribs as he watched those dots pulse like a heartbeat.

They disappeared.

Appeared again.

Disappeared.

He could picture her so clearly—biting her lower lip the way she did when choosing between options, probably typing and deleting a dozen responses. Starting sentences and stopping, like words were photographs she needed to compose perfectly before sharing.

The dots appeared again. Stayed longer this time.

A message appeared: *I remember*

Then, before he could process that, another: *He helped you sleep during the thunderstorm*

She remembered. Not just the laugh but the story he'd told after, about the summer he was ten and terrified of storms and Guardian was the only thing that helped. About his mother being at the hospital and his father traveling for a conference and his aunt letting him bring every stuffed animal he owned into bed. His throat felt tight.

He was typing a response when another message appeared: *Can't sleep either*

Then the dots again, dancing for so long he wondered what novel she was writing and deleting. Finally: *I see you*

She must mean his light under the door.

Another text: *Tomorrow?*

One word that held everything. A question and a promise and maybe, if he was reading it right, the same kind of hope that was currently making it hard to breathe. The room felt too small suddenly, too warm despite the December chill pressing at the windows.

He typed back: *Tomorrow*

Then, because he was exhausted and brave in the way only the sleep-deprived could be: *Sweet dreams, Kelsey*

The dots appeared one more time. Disappeared. Appeared.

You too, Marcus

Not "Dr. Chen" like she'd called him at first, like everybody called him, all professional distance. Not "Chen" like she'd switched to by day two, trying for casual. Marcus. His name in her text was almost as good as hearing her say it. He remembered how she'd said it in October, soft and wondering, like she was trying out how it felt.

Tomorrow, they'd have to talk. Have to figure out what two months of silence meant, what three days early meant, what "I see you" at midnight really meant.

He should shower. Should sleep. Should do anything but sit here staring at his phone screen like it held the secrets of the universe. His body was finally crashing properly—limbs heavy, eyes burning, that disconnected feeling where thoughts moved like honey.

He left Guardian on the pillow where he belonged and headed to the bathroom. The water was too hot but he stood under it anyway, letting it wash away the highway and the hospital and everything except the quiet hope that tomorrow might be different. That tomorrow might be the beginning of something instead of another ending.

When he finally crawled into bed, clean and exhausted beyond measure, he could still see her shadow against his closed eyelids. Could still feel the weight of her name in his mouth.

Tomorrow.

Chapter Five

Kelsey had already changed clothes twice when she heard footsteps in the hallway outside her room. Her heart jumped—Marcus?—before she recognized Agnes's distinctive stride heading toward the stairs.

Eight-thirty. The inn was waking up, which meant she couldn't hide much longer.

She looked at her phone one more time, thumb hovering over their conversation from last night. She'd read it so many times the words had started to lose meaning, except for the last three:

Sweet dreams, Kelsey

Her name. Not "Winters" like he'd called her at first, all professional distance. Not the casual "Hey you" that would have meant nothing. Her actual name, soft and careful like it mattered.

She grabbed her third outfit choice—dark jeans, grey sweater, the kind of unremarkable clothes that said "I definitely didn't spend half an hour thinking about this."

The Dune Walker's Room had opinions about her anxiety. The lighthouse book had somehow migrated from the dresser to her nightstand overnight, falling open to a page about beacon patterns. Her favorite lens cap had rolled under the bed twice, forcing her to get on hands and knees to retrieve it.

"I'm going to breakfast," she announced to the empty room, loading her camera bag with more equipment than any reasonable person needed for interior photography, especially when today wasn't even the big day. Two camera bodies. Four lenses. External flash she'd never use. If she was going to face Marcus Chen over coffee and small talk, she was going armed.

The hallway was quiet, that particular morning hush of a place holding its breath before the day begins. She could hear distant kitchen sounds—someone humming, pans clattering, the homey chaos of breakfast in motion. Her stomach suddenly remembered hunger existed.

The dining room doors were propped open. Morning light streamed through the tall windows, just as it had Monday, but now the space felt different—

charged with pre-wedding energy. White ribbons already graced the doorways, and someone had started placing evergreen boughs along the sideboard.

The smell wrapped her in a warm hug: cinnamon rolls fresh from the oven, bacon crisping somewhere nearby, coffee strong enough to raise the dead. Her usual corner table from Monday beckoned—the one by the window where she could watch everything while seeming absorbed in her camera.

But it was set for two.

"Not there, dear." Beatrice appeared at her elbow, flour dusting her elbow. "Family sits in the kitchen," Beatrice continued, already steering Kelsey toward the swinging door. "The dining room's for guests."

"I am literally a guest," Kelsey protested weakly, but Beatrice was already pushing through the door into a completely different world.

Where the dining room had been all polished formality, the kitchen was pure working heart. Copper pots hung from beams darkened with age and cooking smoke. Herbs dangled in bunches from the ceiling— rosemary, thyme, lavender? The windows were fogged with steam from something wonderful happening on the massive vintage stove, and the whole space smelled like bread and comfort and home.

A scarred wooden table dominated the center, the kind that had seen decades of kneaded dough and chopped vegetables and family conversations. Agnes sat at the head like a general reviewing battle plans, newspaper spread before her and reading glasses perched on her nose. She made notes in margins with decisive pen strokes.

"Coffee consumption in this country," she muttered, not looking up, "is a plague upon proper nutrition."

Cordelia, the youngest sister at what Kelsey guessed was mid-forties, looked up from where she was performing origami miracles with cloth napkins. "Good morning, sunshine! Oh, you look tired. Didn't you sleep?"

Before Kelsey she could say anything in response, Beatrice was guiding her to a chair at the long table. Not just any chair—one that put her between Cordelia's cheerful chatter and an conspicuously empty spot that had place setting but no occupant.

"Sit, sit. Three days, and you're still too thin."

"I eat—"

"Coffee isn't food, young lady." Beatrice was already loading a plate with eggs, bacon, what looked like homemade biscuits. "Agnes, tell her about proper nutrition."

Agnes looked up from her paper, studied Kelsey with the kind of gaze that probably made grown men confess to crimes they didn't commit. "The Chen boy has the same problem. All coffee, no substance. It's a wonder either of you can function."

Kelsey's pulse jumped at the casual mention. She focused on the plate Beatrice set before her—enough food for three people, arranged with the kind of care that made refusal impossible.

"Speaking of Marcus," Cordelia said, folding another napkin swan with impossible dexterity, "he should be down soon. Early riser, that one. Unlike some people." She shot a meaningful look at another empty chair.

"Where's Ella?" Kelsey asked, desperate to shift focus from Marcus and her apparent lack of proper eating habits.

"In the office, poor dear," Beatrice said, refilling a coffee cup Kelsey didn't remember emptying. "Wedding tomorrow, rehearsal tonight, and she's convinced something's going to go wrong. Been up since five making lists."

As if summoned, Ella appeared in the doorway looking exactly as described—beautifully frazzled, carrying two clipboards and a tablet and wearing a sweater that had seen better days. Her hair was twisted up with what appeared to be a pencil, and there was a smudge of ink on her cheek.

"Oh good, you're up!" She collapsed into a chair with the grace of someone running on pure determination. "I have so much to—Beatrice, you're an angel." This last as coffee appeared before her like magic.

"Eat," Agnes commanded, not looking up from her paper. "Can't coordinate on anxiety alone."

"I ate," Ella protested weakly.

"When?" Beatrice demanded.

"Recently. Yesterday. Time is a construct." But she accepted the plate Beatrice prepared, shooting Kelsey a commiserating look. "They do this to everyone. Resistance is futile."

The kitchen door burst open before Kelsey could respond, admitting a whirlwind of snow and energy.

Katie Carter had her brother's eyes but none of his careful reserve—she moved like someone who'd never met a room she couldn't light up. Snow still clung to her sandy hair, and she carried boxes that looked too heavy for her frame.

"Sorry I'm late! The snow made Main Street a skating rink and—oh!" Her eyes landed on Kelsey, brightening with the particular interest artists showed when recognizing their own kind. "You must be the photographer! Ella said you were coming but I didn't realize—is that a vintage Leica?"

Kelsey's hand went automatically to the camera around her neck. "1954 M3. You know cameras?"

"I know art." Katie set her boxes down with a

thump that made Agnes frown over her newspaper. "I work in metal, but I appreciate anyone who captures light. We should talk. Do you ever photograph industrial processes? I've been wanting someone to document the welding—"

"Katie," Ella interrupted gently, "breathe. Coffee first, then artistic collaboration."

Katie laughed, snagging the chair across from Kelsey, between Agnes and Ella. "Sorry. I get excited. It's just rare to find another artist who—"

The kitchen door opened again, more quietly this time.

The cheerful chaos of the kitchen seemed to pause, like everyone took a collective breath. Even the bubbling on the stove quieted to a simmer.

"—understands that capturing a moment is about more than just—oh. Morning, Marcus."

Kelsey's coffee cup froze halfway to her mouth.

He stood in the doorway like he wasn't sure of his welcome, hair still damp from a shower, wire-rimmed glasses slightly fogged from the kitchen's warmth. The navy henley he wore looked soft and well-worn, the kind of shirt someone reached for when they wanted comfort and knew they'd be around family only.

In daylight, he looked different than her midnight imaginings. More real. The kitchen light caught the shadows under his eyes. He looked younger somehow, vulnerable in a way that made her chest tight. But also solid, present, here in a way that late-night texts couldn't capture.

His gaze swept the room, paused on her, and then focused very intently on the coffee pot.

"Morning," he said, voice scratchy despite the apparent shower.

"Sit," Agnes commanded without looking up. "Coffee's hot. Beatrice made biscuits."

The only empty chair was the one next to Kelsey.

Of course.

Marcus moved with the careful precision of someone very aware of their body in space. He pulled out the chair, sat without making it scrape. This close, she could smell him—soap and something green like pine, but underneath that, the faint scent of the lavender sachet she remembered from the inn's linen closets. He smelled like he belonged here.

Their fingers brushed.

Heat shot up her arm like she'd touched a live wire. Her pulse jumped so hard she was sure everyone could see it in her throat. Both jerked back, the coffee pot wobbling between them.

"Sorry—"

"Go ahead—"

"No, you—"

Her face burned. She could feel the flush spreading down her neck, probably clashing horribly with her grey sweater. His hand had been warm, and steadier than hers.

Katie watched this performance with undisguised delight. "Oh, this is adorable."

"Katie," Ella warned.

"What? They're being adorable. Look at them, they can't even pour coffee without—"

"Do you two know each other?" Cordelia asked innocently, though her eyes sparkled with something that suggested the question wasn't innocent at all.

"October," Kelsey and Marcus said simultaneously, then looked at each other in surprise at the synchronized response.

"Ohhhhh," Katie drew out the word, grinning like Christmas had come early. "You're that Kelsey. The one who—" Ella's foot connected with Katie's shin under the table. Katie yelped.

"Violence," Agnes observed mildly, turning a page. "At the breakfast table. What is this family coming to?"

"I was just going to say," Katie continued, rubbing her shin, "the one who took those amazing lighthouse photos. Ella showed me. The way you captured the light was—"

"Thank you," Kelsey managed, hyperaware of Marcus carefully pouring coffee, careful not to look at her, careful everything.

Beatrice set a plate in front of him with the same determined care she'd shown Kelsey. "Eat. Both of you. Can't work on empty stomachs."

"Work?" Marcus asked, finally meeting Kelsey's gaze.

Ella consulted one of her clipboards. "Right. Today's assignments. I need detail shots of all the ceremony spaces—parlor, library, the terrace if the snow stops. Kelsey, you're on photography obviously. Katie, you're on decorations."

"And Marcus," Katie added with suspicious innocence, "can help with the high places. Garlands and such. Placing the lights for the shots. Unless you have other plans?"

"I... no. No plans."

"Perfect!" Ella made a note. "Kelsey, do you mind if Marcus helps? I know you usually work alone, but some of these installations need height, and—"

"It's fine," Kelsey said quickly, not looking at him. "I mean, if he doesn't mind—"

"I don't mind," Marcus said to his coffee cup.

Katie looked between them with the expression of someone watching an excellent tennis match. "This is going to be fun."

"Katie," Ella sighed, "please don't—"

"What? I'm not doing anything. I'm just saying it'll be fun. Working together. Decorating. Nothing else. Why, what did you think I meant?"

Agnes folded her newspaper with decisive precision. "If you're all quite finished with whatever this is, some of us have actual work to do. Beatrice, we need to discuss tomorrow's menu. Cordelia, those centerpieces won't arrange themselves. And you," she pointed at Ella, "need to eat something before you faint."

"I don't faint," Ella protested.

"Eat," Agnes, Beatrice, and Cordelia said in unison.

The kitchen erupted into its usual controlled chaos —multiple conversations, dishes clattering, the comfortable noise of people who'd worked together so long they moved like dancers. Kelsey found herself relaxing despite sitting six inches from Marcus Chen and the way he smelled like soap and snow and something sweet that made her want to lean closer.

Every bit of the breakfast was delicious. Kelsey was shocked to find her plate empty.

"So," Katie said, spreading jam on a biscuit with artistic precision, "the parlor first? I've got all the ribbons and flowers in there already. Just need to make it magical."

"How magical are we talking?" Kelsey asked,

grateful for professional focus. "Understated elegance or—"

"Oh, full fairy tale. Ella wants it to look like Sarah's wedding photos from the fifties. All romantic and glowy and—"

"And achievable by humans," Ella interjected. "Not actual magic. Just... magic-adjacent."

Marcus made a sound that might have been a laugh. Kelsey glanced at him, found him hiding a smile behind his coffee cup. Their eyes met for a second before both looked away.

"Right," Katie said, clearly biting her tongue so as not to say more. "So. Shall we?"

She stood, gathering empty plates with efficient movements. Marcus rose to help, reaching for Kelsey's plate at the same moment she moved to hand it to him.

Another brush of fingers. This time she was ready for it, but that made it worse—the anticipation, the split second of contact, the way her whole body seemed to lean toward him without her permission. Her breath caught, skin prickling with awareness..

"I can—"

"Let me—"

"It's fine—"

Agnes looked up from inspecting a silver tea set for spots. "Children," she said mildly, "the parlor won't decorate itself. Perhaps less stuttering and more doing?"

Heat flooded Kelsey's face. She grabbed her camera bag, needing the familiar weight of equipment. Marcus cleared plates with mechanical precision. Neither looked at the other.

"After you," he said quietly at the kitchen door.

"I need to get another lens from my room—"

"The 35mm is perfect for interiors," he said, then looked surprised at himself. "I mean. I remember from October. You said—"

"Right. Yes. The 35mm."

They stood there, frozen in the doorway, until Katie physically pushed past them. "Parlor. Now. Before Agnes decides we need supervision."

Kelsey followed Katie through the swinging door, hyperaware of Marcus behind her, of the way the morning light caught in his glasses, of how "tomorrow" had become "today" and she had no idea what to do with any of it.

The parlor doors loomed ahead, promising hours of forced proximity and careful choreography around each other.

"After you," Marcus said again at the parlor threshold, and something in his voice made her look back.

He was smiling, just slightly—the same careful smile from October when she'd made him laugh about something ridiculous. When things had been simpler. Before lighthouses and kisses and two months of silence.

"Together?" she suggested, surprising herself.

His smile widened. "Together."

They walked through the doors side by side, Katie already inside exclaiming about ribbon colors.

Maybe—maybe—today might be survivable after all.

Chapter Six

The parlor doors swooshed open like a theater curtain, revealing a space that belonged in a different century. Kelsey immediately started cataloguing the light—morning sun streaming through tall windows topped with stained glass transoms, casting jeweled patterns across the Persian rug. Dust motes danced in the rainbow beams like tiny celebrations.

"Oh," she breathed, already reaching for her camera.

The walls were pale blue, the color of winter sky just before snow, with white crown molding so intricate it looked like carved lace. A massive fireplace dominated one wall, its mantel carved with roses and ivy so realistic Kelsey half-expected them to bloom. Above it hung a portrait of a woman in 1920s dress, her knowing smile suggesting she'd seen every romance that had ever played out in this room.

"That's Ella's great-grandmother," Marcus said quietly beside her. "Elizabeth. She built this room for weddings."

His voice so close made her skin prickle with awareness. She could feel the warmth of him, just inches away, and had to focus on steadying her camera.

"You know the history?"

"Aunt Mei-Lin tells stories." He moved past her into the room, and she caught herself tracking the movement, the easy grace that seemed at odds with his careful, studied behavior. "She says Elizabeth believed every love story deserved a beautiful stage."

The room certainly qualified. Kelsey raised her camera, framing the way light fell across polished hardwood floors at the edges of the carpet. The scent of lemon oil mixed with something floral—ghost roses from a hundred years of bouquets. Beneath that, the comfortable smell of old wood and older stories.

Katie had already claimed the center of the room, surrounded by boxes that seemed to multiply when nobody was looking. White ribbons spilled across three short rows of two dozen white folding lawn chairs, and roses in three shades of ivory filled buckets with casual abundance.

The two matching velvet sofas upholstered and that

big glass coffee table had been banished—hauled onto the porch and covered with tarps. The two stuffed armchairs had been allowed to stay, but were shoved in the back corners, behind the rows of folding chairs.

"Right," Katie announced, hands on hips. "We need swags along all the windows, garland on the mantel, and these little ribbon things on every chair. Ella wants it to look like—" she consulted a photo on her phone "—this, but more."

Kelsey studied the image—Sarah's 1952 wedding, all romantic excess and impossible beauty. "That's a lot of flowers."

"That's a lot of everything," Marcus observed. "Do we have a ladder?"

"Don't need one. That's why you're here, tall person." Katie thrust a bundle of ribbon at him. "You're on high places. Kelsey needs to photograph as we go, so she'll direct. I'll handle the artistic vision."

"I thought Kelsey was handling the artistic vision," Marcus said.

"I'm documenting the artistic vision," Kelsey clarified.

"Right. So I'm just—"

"Tall," Katie and Kelsey said together, then looked at each other in surprise.

Marcus sighed. "Great. Reduced to my height. My mother would be so proud."

"Your mother is five-foot-two," Katie pointed out. "She'd be thrilled you got your dad's genes."

Something flickered across Marcus's face—not quite pain, but close. Kelsey found herself wanting to ask, to smooth away whatever shadow had crossed his features, then remembered they weren't at that level. They were at the "can barely pour coffee without combusting" level.

"Where do we start?" she asked instead, adjusting her camera settings for the tricky light.

Katie pointed to the windows. "Swags first. Marcus, you'll need to—actually, Kelsey, can you show him? I need them draped just so."

And that's how Kelsey found herself standing too close to Marcus Chen, trying to demonstrate ribbon draping while maintaining professional distance and not thinking about how he smelled like her favorite coffee shop back in Chicago.

"Like this," she said, reaching up to show the angle. "See how it should curve?"

"I see how you want it to curve," he said, taking the ribbon. His fingers brushed hers in the transfer, and she felt the contact all the way to her toes. "Whether it will actually curve that way is another question."

"It's ribbon. It doesn't have opinions."

"Everything in this inn has opinions." He stretched to hook the ribbon over the curtain rod, his henley riding up to reveal a strip of skin that made her mouth go dry. She forced herself to look away, but not before noticing the subtle definition of muscle, the way his jeans sat low on his hips. "Including the ribbon."

He was right. The ribbon seemed determined to twist the wrong way, tangle, or simply fall off the moment they looked away. What should have been a five-minute task stretched into fifteen, with Kelsey directing and Marcus following instructions with the focused intensity of someone suturing cardiac tissue.

"A little higher on the left—no, your other left—"

"I know which is left. I went to medical school."

"Could've fooled me. It's still crooked."

"It's artistic."

"It's listing like a sinking ship."

He turned to argue, and suddenly they were closer than intended, her looking up, him looking down, and for a moment neither of them breathed. The deep brown eyes behind his glasses, the double-thick eyelashes. His gaze dropped to her mouth, and she realized she was biting her lip. Again.

Katie's voice broke the spell: "You two are adorable when you bicker."

"We're not bickering," they said in unison, jerking apart. Kelsey's skin felt too hot, like she'd been standing too close to a fire.

"Right. And I don't set things on fire for a living."

Katie held up a rose. "Speaking of which, Marcus, I need your opinion on flower placement. Kelsey's documenting, so she can't have opinions yet."

"I always have opinions," Kelsey muttered, but she raised her camera to capture Marcus's expression as Katie thrust flowers at him.

What followed was twenty minutes of the most ridiculous flower arrangement debate Kelsey had ever witnessed. Marcus, it turned out, had strong feelings about systematic organization. Katie had equally strong feelings about artistic flow. And Kelsey discovered that photographing Marcus's increasingly frustrated expressions was far more entertaining than it should be.

"You can't group them by size," Katie was saying, rearranging his careful work. "This isn't a medical inventory."

"There's nothing wrong with order. Kelsey, tell her."

Kelsey lowered her camera. "Don't drag me into this. I'm Switzerland."

"Switzerland would organize by size," Marcus insisted. "They're very orderly."

"Switzerland would organize by what looks good," Katie countered. "They have excellent taste."

"That's Italy."

"That's everywhere that isn't your hospital."

From behind her camera, Kelsey watched Marcus's face transform with indignation, then amusement, then something softer when he caught her photographing him. He held her gaze through the lens, and her finger trembled on the shutter.

They were reaching for the same white rose when it happened. Three hands, one flower, and suddenly Kelsey was very aware that Marcus's fingers were warm against hers and that Katie had gone suspiciously quiet.

"Sorry," Marcus said, not pulling away immediately. His thumb brushed her knuckle, possibly by accident, and her whole arm tingled.

"It's fine," Kelsey managed, also not pulling away. She could feel his pulse through his fingertips, quick and not quite steady.

"You should take it," he said quietly.

"We could share," she heard herself say. "For the center arrangement."

"I need coffee," Katie announced brightly. "You two keep working. Together. On the flowers. Together."

She practically skipped from the room, leaving them alone with too many flowers and not enough space.

"She's not subtle," Marcus observed, carefully selecting another rose. His ears were slightly pink, which Kelsey found unreasonably endearing.

"None of them are." Kelsey fiddled with the manual settings on her camera. "I think they have a betting pool."

"On what?"

She looked up, found him closer than expected, close enough to see the gold flecks in his brown eyes behind his glasses. "Nothing. Never mind."

They worked in silence for a few minutes, finding a rhythm. He'd place flowers, she'd adjust them slightly, he'd step back for her to photograph. It was almost comfortable, this wordless dance, until their hands brushed again reaching for ribbon.

"We have to stop doing that," Kelsey said, her voice breathier than intended.

"Doing what?"

"The—" she gestured vaguely "—hand thing."

"The hand thing." His mouth twitched like he was fighting a smile. "Very technical term."

"Shut up."

"I didn't say anything."

"You were thinking it."

"You don't know what I'm thinking."

She looked at him directly then, camera temporarily forgotten. "You're thinking this is ridiculous. Two adults who can't manage basic flower arranging without acting like teenagers."

"Actually," he said slowly, his voice dropping to something more intimate, "I was thinking you bite your lip when you're concentrating. On a shot. On an arrangement. On a touch."

Heat flooded her face, pooled low in her stomach. "I don't—"

"Lower left corner. Every time you're framing something important." He turned back to the flowers, but she caught the way his hands weren't quite steady. "Also when you're nervous."

She was definitely biting her lip now. Made herself stop. "I'm not nervous."

"No?"

"No."

"Good." He handed her a rose, careful not to let their fingers touch, but his eyes lingered on her face. "Neither am I."

They were both lying, and they both knew it, but something about acknowledging it made the air lighter. Kelsey raised her camera again, capturing the way morning light caught on crystal vases, the ribbon finally draping properly, the soft chaos of wedding preparation.

"Tell me about the lighthouses," Marcus said suddenly.

Her finger froze on the shutter. "What about it?"

"You're photographing them. Professionally. That's new since October."

"It's not new. I've always—" She stopped, realizing he was right. In October, she'd been doing general freelance work. The lighthouse project had started after.

Because of.

"Michigan Historical Society. They hired me to document all the Great Lakes lighthouses before..." She shrugged. "Before they're gone."

"They're not going anywhere."

"Everything goes somewhere eventually." The words came out sharper than intended. "Sorry. I just mean— things change. Decay. Better to capture them now."

He was quiet for a long moment, adjusting a particularly stubborn piece of baby's breath. When he spoke, his voice was gentle. "Is that why you photograph everything? To keep it from leaving?"

The question hit too close. Kelsey busied herself with changing lenses, though the 35mm was perfect for the current light. "We should finish the mantel. Katie will be back soon."

"Kelsey—"

"The garland needs to go up first, then the flowers." She was already moving away, grabbing greenery from Katie's supplies. "Can you reach without a ladder?"

He studied her for a moment, and she could feel him deciding whether to push. October Marcus would have retreated immediately. This Marcus, tired and raw from whatever had driven him here through a snowstorm, seemed different.

But he just said, "I can reach," and came to help with the garland.

They worked on the mantel in careful cooperation,

Kelsey directing the drape of greenery while Marcus provided height and steady hands. The portrait of Elizabeth watched over them, her painted eyes seeming amused by their careful dance.

"She looks like Sarah," Kelsey observed, photographing the way light and shadow played across the painting.

"Same eyes. Aunt Mei-Lin says all the Thompson women have those eyes. Like they can see straight through you."

"Did you know Sarah well?"

"Well enough." He adjusted the garland's center point. "She used to sneak me cookies when my aunt wasn't looking. Said growing boys needed sugar more than lectures about nutrition."

Kelsey smiled, imagining a younger Marcus being spoiled by the inn's matriarch. "How often did you visit?"

"Summers, mostly. Some holidays." His voice went carefully neutral. "Less after high school."

There was a story there, but before Kelsey could decide whether to ask, Beatrice's voice carried from the kitchen: "Coffee break! I don't care what you're doing, you need proper sustenance!"

"We should go," Marcus said quickly. "Before she comes looking."

But Kelsey was already packing her camera, grateful

for the interruption. The parlor felt too intimate suddenly, all soft light and shared stories and the dangerous warmth of working well together.

They walked to the kitchen in silence, the careful space between them somehow louder than words. But when Marcus held the door for her, his fingers brushed her back so lightly she might have imagined it.

Except for the way her skin burned through her sweater, electric and awake and terrified of what that meant.

The kitchen was empty except for Beatrice, who took one look at them and smiled like she knew secrets. "Sit. Eat. You've been working hard."

She bustled away before either could protest, leaving them alone with coffee and the kind of silence that begged to be filled.

"I wasn't sure you'd come," Kelsey said finally, surprising herself with the honesty.

Marcus looked up from his mug. "To get coffee?"

"To the wedding." She traced the wood grain on the table, not meeting his eyes. "Early."

"I wasn't sure either," he admitted. "Until I was driving."

"What changed?"

He was quiet so long she thought he wouldn't answer. Then: "Thursday got closer."

The simplicity of it made her chest tight. She'd

driven through the night for the same reason—because Thursday meant seeing him, and not seeing him had become harder than facing whatever this was.

"I thought about texting you," he continued, surprising her. "About fifty times. Had whole conversations typed out."

"Why didn't you?"

He smiled ruefully. "What was I supposed to say? 'Hi, I can't stop thinking about October'? 'The lighthouse turned on when we kissed and I dream about it'? 'I miss someone I knew for five days'?"

Each admission hit her like a physical touch. "I would have answered."

"What would you have said?"

She met his eyes finally. "That I missed you too. That I photograph every lighthouse looking for the one that felt like ours. That a couple of days isn't supposed to change everything but—"

"But it did," he finished softly.

"Yeah. It did."

They sat there, looking at each other across the scarred wooden table, and Kelsey felt something shift between them. Not fixed, not solved, but acknowledged. Real.

"Kelsey—"

"Found you!" Katie burst through the door like

sunshine incarnate. "Ready for round two? The library awaits!"

Kelsey stood too quickly, needing distance from the conversation they'd been in the middle of. "Different camera for the library. I should—"

"Actually," Marcus said, standing more slowly, "I promised my aunt I'd help with something. But tonight —" He paused, seemed to gather courage. "The weather's supposed to clear. Stars."

"Stars," Kelsey repeated, heart doing something complicated.

"If you want. The beach path is pretty in snow. Agnes said the Forest Service Caterpillar came by, so it's plowed." He rubbed the back of his neck. "I know it's probably too cold, and you might have plans, but I thought—"

"Yes."

He blinked. "Yes?"

"Yes." She felt reckless, brave, terrified. "Eight o'clock?"

His whole face transformed with a smile that made her knees weak. "Eight o'clock."

Katie's eyes ping-ponged between them with undisguised glee. "Did you just—are you—"

"Katie!" Ella appeared in the doorway, looking harried. "I need you. Ribbon emergency."

"There's no such thing as a—"

"Katie. Now."

Katie allowed herself to be dragged away, but not before shooting Kelsey a look that clearly said "FINALLY."

Leaving them alone again. Always leaving them alone, as if the inn itself was conspiring.

"So," Marcus said, and she could see his pulse jumping at his throat. "Tonight."

"Tonight," she agreed.

They stood there, smiling at each other like idiots, until Agnes's voice carried from somewhere above: "If you're quite finished mooning over each other, some of us have work to do!"

Heat flooded both their faces. Marcus backed toward the door. "I should—my aunt—"

"Right. Yes. Go."

He paused at the threshold. "Eight o'clock."

"You said that already."

"Worth repeating." Another smile, softer this time. "Wear something warm. And Kelsey?"

"Yeah?"

"I'm really glad you came early."

Then he was gone, leaving Kelsey alone with her racing heart and the certainty that she'd just agreed to something that would change everything.

Again.

The kitchen door swung open, admitting Katie's

beaming face. "So? What happened? Did he—did you—stars?"

"Stars," Kelsey confirmed weakly.

Katie actually clapped. "I knew it! Ella owes me twenty bucks."

"You were betting?"

"Of course we were betting. Agnes had Monday, Beatrice said Sunday, but I knew—Friday night stars. Classic Marcus move."

"Classic?"

"Oh, he used to take all the summer kids to see stars. Back when he was a teenager, before—" Katie's expression shifted. "Before things got complicated with his family."

Another piece of the Marcus puzzle, filed away to examine later. Right now, Kelsey had more pressing concerns. "I need to change cameras. And maybe clothes. Do I need different clothes for stargazing? What does one wear to—"

"Breathe," Katie advised, grinning. "It's just stars. And Marcus. And unresolved romantic tension under the winter sky."

"You're not helping."

"I'm not trying to help. I'm trying to win the second bet."

"What second bet?"

Katie's grin widened. "Wouldn't you like to know."

She danced away before Kelsey could respond, leaving her alone with the knowledge that in four hours, she'd be walking in the snow with Marcus Chen, looking at stars and pretending her heart wasn't trying to escape her chest.

She made her way back to her room in a daze, barely registering the inn's familiar hallways. Inside the Dune Walker's Room, she set her camera down and moved to the window. The lighthouse stood in the distance, waiting as always.

Movement below caught her eye. Marcus was in the side garden, helping his aunt with something involving the outdoor decorations. As she watched, he paused to readjust his glasses, the gesture so familiar it made her chest ache. Then he looked up, directly at her window, as if he'd felt her watching.

For a moment they just looked at each other across the distance. Then he raised his hand, accompanied by a smile that promised everything.

Eight o'clock.

Her phone buzzed. A text from an unknown number.

In case you were wondering about the second bet—it's about tomorrow. No pressure -Katie

Tomorrow. Saturday. The wedding.

Another text: PS - Marcus looks really good in a suit. Just saying

Kelsey groaned, but she was smiling. Six hours until stars. Two sleeps until she'd see Marcus in formal wear. Approximately five minutes until her heart rate returned to normal.

She picked up her camera, needing the familiar weight, and found herself photographing the view from her window. Not the lighthouse this time, but the garden where Marcus worked, the place where tonight they'd walk, the whole world that suddenly seemed full of possibility instead of endings.

Some lights, she thought, adjusting her focus, were definitely worth waiting for.

Even if the waiting felt like drowning in starlight.

Especially then.

Chapter Seven

Marcus should have known better than to follow his aunt into the inn's private sitting room at two in the afternoon. The decorations outside had been a ruse, meant to lower his barriers.

Nothing good ever happened in the sitting room at two in the afternoon. That was when Mei-Lin did her serious thinking, her planning, her gentle manipulation disguised as concern.

But he'd been lulled by the morning's success, by Kelsey saying yes to tonight, by the way working beside her had felt like coming home to a place he'd never lived. So when his aunt said she needed help with the tea service setup, he'd followed without thinking.

The door clicked shut behind him with the finality of a trap springing.

"Sit," Mei-Lin said. She pointed to one of the two straight-backed velvet-padded chairs with the narrow arms as she sat in the other.

She had his cellphone in her hand.

His stomach dropped. "Aunt Mei-Lin—"

"Seven missed calls." She set the phone on the small lace-covered Victorian table between them like evidence in a trial. "Your mother is concerned."

Marcus sank into the chair across from her, recognizing the setup. The sitting room was Mei-Lin's domain—all thick carpets and carved wooden screens, a blend of her Chinese heritage and Michigan practicality. Afternoon light filtered through lace curtains, casting patterns that looked like judgment.

"She's always concerned," he said carefully.

"This time with reason. You drove through a snowstorm on no sleep. You haven't answered her calls. She used the word 'erratic.'"

"Since when is coming to visit family erratic?"

Mei-Lin's look could have stripped paint. "Since when do you come to family without six weeks' notice and a detailed itinerary?"

She had a point. Marcus slumped deeper into the chair, which smelled like the lavender sachets his aunt tucked everywhere. "What did she want?"

"Besides reassurance that you haven't lost your mind?" Mei-Lin poured tea from a pot that had appeared from nowhere, her movements precise as surgery. "She mentioned the Whitmore position."

There it was. Marcus accepted the tea—chrysanthemum, for cooling hot tempers—and tried to keep his face neutral. "Chief Matthews isn't retiring until spring."

"The board wants to meet candidates early. Your mother has spoken to them about you."

"Of course she has."

"They want you to fly out next week. An informal meeting, she called it." Mei-Lin's tone suggested she knew exactly how informal Helena Chen's informal meetings were. "During Christmas season."

"Emergencies don't take holidays," Marcus recited automatically, then caught himself. His mother's words in his mouth, like always.

"Neither does family," Mei-Lin countered. "Yet here you are, choosing one over the other."

"I haven't chosen anything. I haven't even finished residency."

"Your mother has it all planned out. The position, the advancement track, the research opportunities." She sipped her tea, watching him over the rim. "Even the appropriate living arrangements near the hospital."

Marcus set his cup down harder than necessary. "She picked out an apartment?"

"A condo. Good investment potential."

He laughed, but it came out bitter. "Of course. God forbid I live somewhere without investment potential."

"Marcus." His aunt's voice gentled. "She loves you. She wants—"

"She wants me to be her." He stood, needing to move. "Chief of Emergency Medicine by forty. Published research. Respected. Alone."

"She's not alone."

"Name one relationship she's had that lasted longer than her surgical residency."

Mei-Lin was quiet for a long moment, waiting for him to remember.

"She had your father."

"And pushed him away with both hands the moment he suggested she might work less than eighty hours a week." Marcus moved to the window, looking out at the snow-covered garden. "I watched it happen. Watched her choose the hospital over school concerts, over anniversaries, over everything."

"And you're afraid you're like her."

He turned, surprised by the directness. But this was Mei-Lin. She didn't deal in gentle deflections when truth would do.

"I am like her," he admitted. "Same hands. Same

drive. Same inability to—" He stopped, thinking of Kelsey in the parlor, the way she'd said they kept doing 'the hand thing' like touch was dangerous. The way his whole body had responded to that brief contact, like being shocked back to life.

"Same inability to what?"

"To stay," he finished quietly. "To choose people over achievement. To believe something matters more than the next save, the next accomplishment."

Mei-Lin rose, moved to stand beside him at the window. "You came here. That's choosing."

"I came here exhausted and half-broken because I lost a patient. That's not choosing, that's running."

"Is it?" She touched his shoulder gently. "Or is it running to instead of running from?"

Before he could answer, she was moving toward the door. "The Winters girl is in the library, photographing old albums. Cordelia is helping her. Perhaps you should make sure they don't find anything too embarrassing."

The subject change was so abrupt it took him a moment to catch up. "Kelsey's looking at albums?"

"Mmm. From the summers. The nineties, I believe." Mei-Lin's expression was too innocent. "Wasn't that when you had that unfortunate haircut?"

"Aunt Mei-Lin—"

But she was already gone, leaving him with cooling tea and the certainty that he'd been managed. He grabbed his phone, seeing the missed calls lined up like accusations. Later. He'd deal with his mother later. Right now, the thought of Kelsey looking at his awkward teenage years was somehow more terrifying than any career decision.

He found them on the second floor, in the library, Cordelia's delighted laughter carrying down the hall like a warning bell. The library door stood open, revealing a room that seemed designed for secrets and quiet revelations.

The space was smaller than the parlor but no less grand—floor-to-ceiling shelves in dark mahogany reached toward a coffered copper ceiling. A bay window created a reading nook with built-in seats covered in worn velvet cushions, the kind that had cradled generations of readers. Winter light filtered through diamond-paned glass, casting geometric shadows across the parquet floor.

The smell hit him like a physical memory—old paper and leather bindings, lemon oil on wood, the faint must of knowledge accumulated over decades. But underneath, something else: vanilla and camera lens cleaner. Kelsey's scent, already claiming space in this room of memories.

She sat cross-legged on the rug near the fireplace, surrounded by albums, her camera temporarily forgotten. Cordelia more wisely was seated in one of the two wingback chairs.

Marcus's breath caught hard in his throat. Kelsey looked utterly at home here, legs folded beneath her, completely absorbed in whatever Cordelia was showing her. The formal photographer's distance she usually maintained had melted away, leaving someone younger, softer, unguarded.

The light from the window caught in her hair, turning dark strands auburn, and when she laughed at something Cordelia said—really laughed, not her polite professional sound—her whole face transformed. Joy looked good on her.

Joy looked devastating on her.

His heart hammered against his ribs as heat flooded through him. Marcus had to grab the doorframe to steady himself from the want that crashed through him. Unexpected. Overwhelming.

"—and this one!" Cordelia was saying, pointing to a photo. "He insisted on wearing that lab coat everywhere. Even to the beach. Said he was conducting 'experiments.'"

"What kind of experiments?" Kelsey asked, and the genuine interest in her voice made Marcus's chest tight.

"Mostly involving sand castles and optimal structural integrity." Cordelia turned the page. "Oh! And here's when he tried to teach the summer kids about constellations but forgot Orion has a belt, not suspenders."

"Okay," Marcus announced from the doorway. "That's enough character assassination for one day."

Kelsey looked up, and the smile on her face made him forget why he'd been embarrassed. "Nice hair," she said, gesturing to a photo. "Very... vertical."

He moved closer, trying to appear casual while his body felt hyperaware of every step that brought him nearer to her. He saw the picture in question—fifteen-year-old Marcus with hair gelled into spikes that defied physics and good taste. "It was the nineties. Everyone looked like that."

"No," Cordelia said cheerfully. "Everyone did not look like that. That was all you, sweetie."

"You look happy," Kelsey observed, studying the photo with the same intensity she brought to her camera work. When she bit her lower lip in concentration, Marcus had to clench his fists to keep from reaching out to trace that gesture. "Happier than—" She stopped, color flooding her cheeks.

"Than what?"

"Than your October photos," she admitted, the blush spreading down her neck. "I may have taken more than I showed you."

His pulse kicked into overdrive. "May have?"

"Definitely did." She turned another page, not

meeting his eyes. "You photograph well when you don't know you're being watched."

The idea of her watching him, capturing moments he hadn't known he was giving away, made heat pool low in his stomach. And then ice. "What kind of moments?"

"The way you furrow your brow when you're concentrating. How you roll your shoulders when you're tense. That half-smile when you think something's funny but don't want to admit it." She glanced up, caught his expression, looked away quickly. "Professional observation."

"Right. Professional."

Cordelia looked between them with obvious delight. "Oh, this is interesting. Tell me more about October."

"Nothing to tell," Marcus said quickly.

"So much nothing that you're both blushing?" Cordelia patted the floor beside her. "Sit. Let me show Kelsey baby Marcus while you tell me lies about October."

He sat, careful to maintain distance from Kelsey, but Cordelia immediately scooted her chair over, forcing them closer. His thigh pressed against Kelsey's, and even through denim he could feel her warmth. She shifted slightly, but that only brought her shoulder against his arm. He caught her quick intake of breath, saw the way her fingers trembled as she turned another album page.

"Now, this album is from 1992. Marcus was seven and convinced the lynx lived in our attic."

"Because Agnes told me it did," Marcus protested, trying to focus on the conversation instead of the way Kelsey smelled like vanilla and lavender and winter mornings.

"Agnes tells everyone that. Most seven-year-olds don't build lynx traps out of yarn and cookie boxes."

Kelsey laughed so hard her shoulder shook against his. "Did you catch anything?"

"A lot of dust. One really mad bat. And Agnes, who was not amused by the cookie theft."

They went through albums, Cordelia providing running commentary that got more embarrassing with each page. But Marcus found it hard to care about the embarrassment when every photo gave him an excuse to lean closer to Kelsey, to point out details, to accidentally brush her arm as they turned pages.

"Why did your mom stop bringing you?" Kelsey asked suddenly, finger paused on a photo of teenage Marcus with Sarah.

The question cut through the warm haze of proximity. Cordelia's laughter died. "That's—"

"Not your story to tell," Marcus finished.

The library went quiet except for the old radiator's gentle hiss. Kelsey looked between them, and he could see her cataloguing the sudden tension, filing it away like she did everything else.

"I should check on the rehearsal setup," Cordelia said, standing with less grace than usual. "You two... enjoy the albums. Be sure to put them back. Marcus knows where they go."

She left them alone with years of memories spread across the floor and questions hanging in the air like dust motes.

"You don't have to explain," Kelsey said quietly.

But suddenly he wanted to. Wanted her to understand. "She wanted me to do summer programs. SAT prep, pre-med enrichment, anything that looked good on applications."

"Instead of coming here."

"Instead of 'wasting time' here." He picked up a photo—him at seventeen, already looking serious, already choosing his path. "My dad fought for my summers. Said I needed to be a kid, not a resume. But by the time I was seventeen..."

"The fighting got old," Kelsey finished. She shifted, and suddenly they were facing each other, knees touching. The contact sent electricity up his spine.

"Yeah. It did. So I chose the path of least resistance. Chose the program. Chose her approval."

"And stopped coming here."

"Until October." He met her eyes, saw his own want reflected there. "I told myself I was too busy. Internships, residencies, all the things that mattered. But really..."

"Really you were afraid coming back would hurt." Her voice dropped to almost a whisper. "Because places can only hurt you if you let them matter."

They sat in the quiet for a moment, his thumb tracing absent patterns on her skin. The library held them in its patient embrace, all these documented lives surrounding them—people who'd chosen to stay, to belong, to matter.

"Is that why you photograph everything?" he asked softly. "To hold onto things without having to stay?"

She turned her hand palm up, their fingers not quite interlacing but close. "Military kid, remember? I learned early not to get attached. Three years was the longest we ever stayed anywhere."

"Must have been hard." He was stroking his thumb across her palm now, feeling her pulse flutter.

"Nah, it was normal. Pack up, move on, start over. Make friends you'll leave, find favorite places you'll forget." Her fingers curled slightly, catching his. "After my dad died, my mom remarried within six months. Another military guy. Like she was just... checking off a box. Starting over again."

"Kelsey—"

"I was fifteen. Old enough to understand she was grieving, not old enough to forgive her for packing up Dad's things like this was just another transfer." She looked up at him, eyes bright with unshed tears. "I learned to leave first after that. Document everything but keep moving. Don't look back. You've got the photos."

Marcus lifted his free hand, brushed a strand of hair behind her ear. Her breath caught.

"But you came back here," he said. "In October. And now."

"So did you."

"Maybe we're both bad at staying away."

She leaned into his touch, just slightly. "Maybe we are."

They were sitting so close now he could see the spray of colors that made up her hazel eyes. Her lips parted, and he found himself leaning in, drawn by something stronger than gravity.

"There you are!" Margaret Carter's voice from the doorway made them spring apart like guilty teenagers. Marcus's whole body protested the loss of contact. "I've been looking everywhere. Marcus, dear, we need you to stand in for the groomsmen at rehearsal. And Kelsey, you'll want to set up your shots, won't you?"

Then she paused. She studied them both, took in the albums spread across the floor, the way they'd put careful distance between themselves but couldn't stop stealing glances.

"Of course," Kelsey said, already reaching for her camera, but Marcus noticed the tremor in her hands. "That's what I'm here for."

"Wonderful." Margaret's smile was warm but knowing. "No rush, though. Rehearsal starts in half an hour. But don't be late."

She left them alone again, but the spell was broken. Kelsey busied herself closing albums, and Marcus helped, both careful not to let their hands touch again. The absence of contact felt like a physical ache.

"I should get ready," she said, standing. "Make sure my equipment is set."

He stood too, stepping closer than necessary. "So tonight..."

"Eight o'clock," she confirmed, clutching albums to her chest like armor. But her eyes kept dropping to his mouth. "Unless you've changed your mind?"

"No. Definitely no." He reached out, tugged one album from her grasp, let his fingers brush hers in the process. Her sharp intake of breath made him bold. "Stars are supposed to be incredible tonight."

"Good. That's... good." She was biting her lip again, and this time he didn't stop himself from reaching out, pressing his thumb gently to her lower lip.

"You're doing it again," he said softly.

"Doing what?" Her words were muffled against his thumb.

"The lip thing. When you're nervous."

"I'm not—" She stopped, seeming to realize she was literally biting her lip while denying it. "Okay. Maybe a little nervous."

"Why?" He let his hand drop but stayed close.

"Because you're looking at me like..." She trailed off.

"Like what?"

"Like you did in October. Right before you kissed me."

The air between them went electric. Marcus leaned in slightly. "Kelsey—"

"I should go," she said quickly, but she swayed toward him instead of away. "Rehearsal. Photos. Equipment."

"Right." But neither of them moved.

They stood there, surrounded by years of documented history, bodies angled toward each other like plants toward sun.

Finally, Kelsey stepped back, looking as shaken as he felt.

"Tonight," she said again, like a promise.

Before he could respond, she was gone. He stood in the library, surrounded by photo albums and golden afternoon light, his thumb still warm from touching her lip.

His phone buzzed. Another call from his mother.

He declined it and bent to gather the albums. He had a rehearsal to get ready for, a part to play in his chosen family's celebration. Tonight he'd walk with Kelsey under stars he'd once used to navigate away from here.

The lighthouse was visible through the library's bay window, dark now but waiting. Always waiting for the right moment to blaze to life.

Eight o'clock couldn't come fast enough.

Chapter Eight

Kelsey made it to her room before her knees gave out. She leaned against the closed door, camera bag sliding from her shoulder, and pressed her fingers to her lips where Marcus had touched them.

You're doing it again.

His voice, low and careful, like she was something that might spook. His thumb, warm and firm, pressing gently against her lower lip. The way his eyes had gone stormy behind his glasses when she'd admitted why she was nervous.

Her whole body still hummed from that touch. Skin too sensitive, like he'd awakened nerve endings she didn't know existed. She pushed off from the door, needing movement, needing something to do with hands that wouldn't stop shaking. The rehearsal started in thirty minutes. She had equipment to check, shots to plan, a professional facade to construct from the rubble of whatever had just happened in the library.

Her camera bag yielded its familiar treasures—the Canon she used for formal shots, the vintage Leica for candids, memory cards organized in their labeled case. She checked batteries, cleaned lenses that were already clean, anything to avoid thinking about the way Marcus had leaned in at the end, the way she'd wanted him to close that distance.

Tonight.

The word thrummed through her like a pulse. Three and a half hours until eight o'clock. Until stars and snow and whatever came next.

She changed clothes quickly—black pants and a cream sweater that was professional enough for photographing a rehearsal but soft enough to be touched. Not that anyone would be touching her. Not that she was thinking about Marcus's hands, the way his thumb had been so gentle, the way his other hand might—

"Stop it," she told her reflection firmly, but her cheeks were flushed, her pupils dilated like she'd already been kissed.

A knock at the door made her jump. "Five minutes,

dear!" Beatrice called. "Everyone's gathering in the parlor!"

The parlor. Right. Where she'd spent the morning trying not to combust every time Marcus reached past her. Where they'd be practicing for tomorrow's ceremony. She could absolutely manage to be in the same room as Marcus Chen without spontaneously combusting.

Absolutely.

After they'd run through everything three times, it was time for dinner.

The parlor had been transformed since morning. In the early evening, what had been charming in daylight now glowed with romantic possibility. Someone had lit the fireplace, flames casting dancing shadows across the walls. Candles flickered on every surface—the mantel they'd decorated, the side tables, even clustered on the floor in glass hurricanes. The afternoon sun was fading, painting everything in gold and amber, making the room feel like the inside of a jewel box.

Their morning's work showed beautifully—white roses and evergreen garlands caught the mixed light, seeming to glow from within. The chairs had been arranged in neat rows facing the fireplace, creating an aisle down the center. It was intimate, romantic, exactly what a wedding should be.

"Oh," Ella breathed beside her. "It's perfect."

She stood in the doorway clutching Liam's hand, her face soft with wonder. He looked at her like she was the only thing in the room worth seeing. Kelsey raised her camera, capturing that moment of pure love.

Through her viewfinder, she saw Liam in sharp detail. The way he'd dressed up for the rehearsal in dark jeans that actually fit properly without a tool belt attached and a navy button-down that Ella had probably picked out. His sleeves were rolled to his forearms in that casually deliberate way that revealed forearms corded with the kind of muscle that came from honest labor. His hair, darker than his father's, had been tamed into submission, though a rebellious wave still fell across his forehead. When he smiled down at Ella, his whole face transformed—those Carter blue eyes warming from their usual careful assessment to something tender and private.

Other arrivals filled the space. Liam's father, Robert Carter stood near the fireplace, checking note cards with the focused attention of someone who took responsibility seriously. At sixty-eight, he commanded the room without trying, his silver hair neatly combed back from a face that had weathered decades of Michigan winters. He wore what Kelsey guessed was his good gray suit—

not quite formal enough for tomorrow but several steps up from what he wore to run Carter & Son Carpentry and Hardware. Even dressed up, his hands gave him away as he shuffled the cards—scarred knuckles and permanent calluses that spoke of a lifetime building things that mattered. When he looked up and smiled at his wife, the stern lines of his face softened into something that made Kelsey understand where Liam had learned to love so completely.

Margaret Carter moved between the chairs with purposeful grace, adjusting already-perfect bows. Her silver hair was styled in elegant waves that caught the candlelight, and she'd chosen a deep plum sweater and pressed charcoal slacks. She had the darker blue eyes than her son, and sharper, like winter sky over the lake. Eyes that missed nothing and catalogued everything. When she murmured something to Katie, her voice carried the particular authority of a mother who'd raised children and knew exactly when to speak and when to let silence do the work.

Katie was adding more candles because apparently there could never be enough. And Marcus, because of course Marcus, helping Agnes with something near the windows.

He'd changed into a button-down shirt, forest green that made his skin glow warm in the mixed light. When he turned and saw her, his whole body stilled. His gaze dropped to her lips, and she knew he was remembering the library too. The air between them crackled with awareness.

Heat flooded through her, pooling low in her stomach. She fumbled her camera, nearly dropping it. His lips quirked in a smile that said he knew exactly what he did to her.

"Places, everyone!" Robert called, his voice carrying the rumble of someone used to being heard over power tools and grandchildren alike, and the spell broke.

Sort of.

Kelsey positioned herself for optimal angles as the wedding party started to walk through their paces. And then stopped.

Patricia Thompson had arrived fashionably late, pausing in the doorway as if steeling herself before entering.

She was a study in controlled elegance—silver-blonde hair cut in a precise bob that moved as one piece, winter white cashmere coat over matching slacks that had never seen a wrinkle. Her face—Ella's face—might have been beautiful if it weren't held so carefully still, as if any expression might crack her perfect facade.

Kelsey didn't know the story behind Ella and her

mom, just that her mom was staying in town, not at the inn.

Which, ow.

Mrs. Thompson moved through the room like someone navigating a minefield of memories, her posture so perfect it looked painful. Everything about her seemed designed to deflect—the neutral colors, the understated jewelry, the way she held herself just slightly apart from the warmth of the room. But her eyes, when they landed on Ella, betrayed her. They were the same warm brown as her daughter's, and for just a moment, just as full of love.

And judgment.

"Ella, darling," she said, kissing her daughter's cheek lightly. "The space is... quaint."

"It's perfect," Ella said firmly, and Liam's hand moved to her back—protective, supportive, his work-roughened fingers gentle against her sweater. Another moment Kelsey captured—the way they stood together against subtle criticism.

Mrs. Thompson's gaze swept the room, lingering on the candles that seemed to flicker in patterns, the roses that smelled too fresh for December, the twinkling everywhere. Her perfectly manicured fingers tightened on her clutch purse.

"Yes, well. The inn always did have its own... atmosphere." The word came out careful, controlled, but Kelsey caught the slight tremor underneath. Not judgment of her daughter's choices, but something closer to fear. Like Patricia was in the presence of something she'd once fled and couldn't quite trust even now.

"Marcus, you'll stand in for groomsmen," Robert directed. "Right here, next to Liam, where Tom will be tomorrow." If Tom—right now Liam's older brother, who did something secret for the government, was a maybe. Marcus might be the permanent stand-in.

Kelsey watched through her lens as Marcus took his position, and her traitor camera seemed determined to focus on him instead of the actual couple. The way the candlelight turned his skin golden. The way he stood with careful attention, like everything mattered. The way his eyes kept flicking to her across the room, dark with promise.

Every time their gazes met, her body responded— pulse jumping, skin flushing, that low ache in her stomach intensifying. She was supposed to be professional, focused, but all she could think about was eight o'clock and stars and what his hands might feel like in her hair.

"Now, we'll run through the processional," Robert continued. "Ella, you'll enter from—"

"Excuse me." Margaret Carter materialized at Kelsey's elbow with the stealth of someone who'd raised children and learned to move through chaos unnoticed. "You're the photographer from October."

It wasn't a question. Kelsey lowered her camera carefully. "Yes, ma'am."

"The one Marcus—Mrs. Frankl's nephew—has been asking about."

Heat flooded Kelsey's face. "I—he has?"

Margaret studied her with those sharp blue eyes. "Mei-Lin mentioned you at tea last week. Said the boy's been different since October. Distracted." Her tone was neutral, but her eyes were charged. "My boys are the same way. When a Carter man falls, he falls hard."

"Mrs. Carter—"

"The question is," Margaret continued smoothly, "are you the catching kind or the letting-go kind?"

Across the room, Marcus was helping Patricia with her chair, carefully polite. His attention kept drifting to their corner, and when he saw Kelsey with Margaret, his expression went wary.

"I don't know," Kelsey admitted, surprising herself with honesty. "I've never been good at staying."

Margaret's expression softened slightly, laugh lines appearing at the corners of her eyes. "Neither was I, dear. Military family. New base every few years. Until I met Robert and realized some things are worth growing roots for."

She patted Kelsey's arm with fingers bare but for a

simple gold band, and moved away, leaving Kelsey reeling. Around her, the rehearsal continued—people moving through patterns, practicing joy. She raised her camera again, but her hands weren't quite steady.

During the practice vows, when Robert read the words about choosing each other daily, about building a life together, Marcus's eyes found hers across the space. The look in them—heat and hope and something deeper—made her whole body flush. She missed the shot of Ella's tearful smile, too lost in imagining those words being said to her, by by someone—by him—in this same candlelit space.

The dining room at evening was a completely different creature than its morning incarnation. Where sunlight had made it cheerful and welcoming, candlelight transformed it into something from a dream. The mahogany furniture gleamed deeper, richer, creating pools of shadow and light. The blue willow china had been replaced with Sarah's formal set—white porcelain with gold rims that caught every flicker of flame.

Candles marched down the center of the table in crystal holders, their light multiplying in the mirror above the sideboard. The whole room smelled of beeswax and roses and the rich food Beatrice had been preparing all day. It was formal without being stuffy, elegant without being cold—like being inside a warm embrace.

Someone—probably Katie—had arranged the seating, and Kelsey found herself between Marcus and Patricia Thompson, which felt like being between temptation and judgment.

Marcus pulled out her chair, his fingers brushing her shoulder in the process. The touch shot through her like lightning, and she had to reach for the table edge to keep from leaning back into his hand.

"You look—" he started quietly, his breath warm against her ear.

"Perfect," she finished, remembering his whisper from earlier. "You said that already."

"Bears repeating." His voice was low, private, despite the room full of people. "Especially after…"

He trailed off, but his eyes half closed, and she knew he was thinking about the library too. About his thumb on her lip, about almost kisses, about the way tonight stretched between them like a promise. Her lips tingled with sense memory, and she bit her lower lip without thinking.

His pupils dilated. "You're doing it again."

"I know," she whispered, and watched his jaw clench.

"Wine?" Katie appeared with suspicious timing, bottle already tipping toward Kelsey's glass.

"Just one," Kelsey managed. "I'm working."

"Sure you are." Katie's grin was knowing. "Working on not staring at—ow!"

Ella's foot had found Katie's shin under the table. "The wine is lovely, thank you."

Conversation flowed around them—Patricia warming up enough to tell sweet stories of Ella's childhood, Robert asking advice on bits of tomorrow's ceremony, the sisters arguing about breakfast timing. Normal rehearsal dinner chaos, except for the way Marcus's knee pressed against hers under the table and neither of them moved away.

The contact burned through two layers of fabric. She was hyperaware of every shift, every breath, every tiny adjustment that brought them closer or farther apart. When he reached for his water glass, his arm brushed hers, and she shivered.

"Cold?" he murmured.

"No." The opposite. She was burning, every nerve ending alive and focused on him.

"Remember when Liam tried to build that raft?" Marcus asked suddenly, voice carrying over the chatter, but his hand found hers under the table as he spoke.

Liam groaned. "We agreed never to speak of the raft."

"You said it was engineeringly sound," Katie added gleefully. "Right before it sank in three feet of water."

"It was sabotage," Liam protested. "Someone loosened the lashings."

"Waves loosened the lashings," Marcus corrected, his thumb stroking over Kelsey's knuckles as he talked. "Very small waves. From minnows."

She was trying to follow the conversation, trying to laugh at the right moments, but Marcus's touch was scrambling her brain. His fingers intertwined with hers, and she had to bite back a sound at how right it felt.

Robert stood, raising his glass. "Before we get too deep into embarrassing stories, I'd like to propose a toast. To Ella and Liam, who remind us daily that love isn't just a feeling—it's a choice, a practice, and sometimes..." He paused, eyes twinkling. "A light that guides us home."

As if on cue, the lighthouse blazed to life outside the windows.

Everyone gasped, turning to look. The beam swept across the water, impossible and brilliant against the winter evening. Plates rattled as people pushed back chairs, moving to the windows for a better view.

"It hasn't done that in years!" Margaret exclaimed.

"Not since—" Agnes started, then stopped, eyes finding Marcus and Kelsey still seated, still holding hands.

"Since October," Katie stage-whispered. "When Marcus and Kelsey—"

Ella's kick must have been more forceful this time because Katie actually yelped.

Marcus hadn't moved, hadn't released Kelsey's hand, hadn't looked away from her face. If anything, his grip had tightened. "Interesting timing," he said quietly.

"Very interesting," she agreed, heart hammering so hard he must be able to hear it.

Around them, people exclaimed over the lighthouse, debated explanations, took photos with their phones. But Marcus and Kelsey sat in their own bubble, hands clasped under the table, that beam of light sweeping over them like a blessing.

At eight o'clock, the lobby was indeed full of people trying very hard to look casual. Beatrice had materialized from the kitchen, now sitting on the tall stool behind the welcome desk with some knitting project. Cordelia was wiping down surfaces that already gleamed. Ella sat organizing place cards that were already in perfect order while Liam stood beside her, obviously wishing for invisibility.

Kelsey made it all but three steps down the wide stairs before Katie skulking by the door, chirped, "Don't you look nice! Perfect for stargazing. Or other activities. Star-adjacent activities."

"Katie," Ella warned.

"What? I'm just saying she looks nice. Marcus will think—oh look, there he is! Marcus, doesn't Kelsey look nice?"

Marcus stood at the bottom of the stairs, and Kelsey forgot how to breathe. He wore dark jeans and a charcoal sweater that made his shoulders look broader, a wool coat over his arm. When he saw her, his whole body went still, like she'd stopped his world.

"Very nice," he agreed, but his voice was rough, and his eyes were doing that thing where they darkened behind his glasses. "Beautiful."

They stood frozen, him three steps down, her three steps up, everyone watching with varying degrees of subtlety. The air between them practically crackled.

"Should we...?" Marcus gestured toward the door.

"Yes. Yep. Let's go. Now."

She descended quickly, and he met, offering his arm. The moment she took it, heat shot through her, even through all the layers of winter clothes. They moved toward the door with probably too much speed, but behind them the commentary had already started.

"Have fun stargazing!" Katie called.

"Bundle up!" Cordelia added. "Body heat helps!"

"The lighthouse is already on," Agnes observed dryly. "In case you needed mood lighting."

Kelsey felt her face flame, but Marcus just opened the door, ushering her into the cold night air. His hand on her lower back burned through her coat. The porch was blissfully empty, snow falling in fat, lazy flakes, the world muffled and perfect.

"They're not subtle," she said.

He took a moment to slide his coat on. Then he offered his arm again, and this time when she took it, he covered her hand with his, warm even through gloves. "Ready to go look at some stars?"

"Even though the lighthouse might upstage them?"

"Let it try." He started down the steps, steadying her when her boot slipped on new snow. "I've got my own light."

It was cheesy and romantic and perfect, and Kelsey found herself laughing, only a little nervously. Behind them, curtains twitched with their audience's attention, but ahead lay the beach path, the promise of stars, and whatever came after eight o'clock on a clear December night.

"Marcus?" she said as they reached the path.

"Mmm?"

"I'm glad you drove through a snowstorm."

His hand tightened on hers. "Me too. Kelsey?"

"Yes?"

"I haven't stopped thinking about the library."

Heat flooded through her. "Me neither."

They walked into the night together, leaving foot-prints in fresh snow, while behind them the inn glowed with warmth and ahead the lighthouse painted silver roads across dark water. And somewhere between here and there, under stars that had watched a thousand love stories, they'd write their own.

Chapter Nine

The path to the beach was a tunnel of quiet, snow muffling their footsteps until each step sounded like a whispered secret. Marcus breathed in air so cold it burned his lungs, sharp with pine and distant woodsmoke from the inn's chimneys. But underneath that—vanilla. Kelsey's shampoo or lotion or just her, the scent stronger in the cold as if winter had concentrated everything about her into something he could taste on each inhale.

"Careful," he said, steadying her as her boot slipped on ice hidden beneath fresh powder. "The path gets tricky here." The quarter-moon gave only just enough light to see by. If clouds came in, he'd have to dig out the flashlights.

"I remember." Her voice carried warmth despite the

cold, and when she glanced up at him, snowflakes caught on her eyelashes like tiny stars. "You caught me in the same spot in October."

He had. Remembered the weight of her against him for that brief moment, how it had felt like holding lightning. Now her arm was linked through his, a constant line of contact that burned through layers of wool and down. Every adjustment, every shift as they navigated the path sent sparks through him.

Sparks that were starting to feel normal.

"Fewer people in October," he said, needing conversation to distract from how badly he wanted to stop walking and kiss her right there in the snow.

She laughed, the sound bright in the winter quiet. "Our audience was subtle."

"Beatrice knitting. Cordelia cleaning. Very subtle."

"Don't forget Katie's commentary on body heat."

"I'm trying to forget that, actually."

The lighthouse beam swept over them, turning the falling snow into a slice of silver light. In that moment, she looked otherworldly—cheeks pink from cold, eyes bright. His free hand clenched in his pocket to keep from reaching for her.

The path opened onto the beach, and they both stopped. The lake stretched endlessly black except where the lighthouse painted silver roads across its surface. Snow had transformed the familiar shoreline into something from a dream—pristine white sand except for their footprints, driftwood wearing caps of snow like sleeping giants. The air here was different, charged with moisture and the mineral scent of winter lake, so cold it made his teeth tingle.

"Oh," Kelsey breathed, and her wonder made him see it fresh. The impossible beauty of this place that had shaped him.

"Come on," he said, tugging her toward a massive log he remembered from childhood summers. "Best stargazing spot on the beach."

His boots crunched through snow, the sound loud in the hushed night. Underneath, frozen sand shifted, and he could hear the lake's quiet conversation with the shore—not quite waves, more like whispered promises. The lighthouse continued its steady rhythm, beam sweeping across them in predictable intervals, marking time.

"You came prepared," Kelsey observed as he pulled a thick wool blanket from his backpack.

"I'm trying to learn." He shook it out, the fabric releasing the scent of cedar from the inn's linen closet. "Hot chocolate?"

"You brought hot chocolate?" Her smile did dangerous things to his composure.

"Aunt Mei-Lin's special recipe. With—"

"Cinnamon," they said together, then laughed.

He spread the blanket over the log, the rough bark catching at the wool. The wood was cold even through the fabric, solid and grounding beneath them as they sat. Close. Not quite touching but almost, the inch between them crackling with possibility.

Marcus poured hot chocolate into the thermos lid, the rich scent mixing with winter air. When he handed it to her, their gloved fingers brushed, and even through leather and wool, heat shot up his arm.

"To stargazing," she said, raising the makeshift cup.

"To stargazing," he agreed, watching her lips touch the rim, leaving the faintest shine of lip gloss behind.

She made a soft sound of pleasure as she tasted it. "Oh, that's perfect. How does she get it so—"

"Secret ingredient," he said, accepting the cup back, deliberately drinking from the same spot. The ghost of her lip gloss, the warmth of where her mouth had been —it was probably his imagination, but he could swear he tasted vanilla beneath the chocolate.

Above them, the winter sky showed off. Without light pollution and with the cold air creating perfect clarity, stars scattered across the darkness like spilled diamonds. The Milky Way was visible as an actual river of light, and Marcus pointed out constellations automatically. Orion standing guard, Cassiopeia lounging in her chair, the Pleiades clustered like gossips.

But he kept losing focus because Kelsey had shifted

closer, their thighs touching through denim. She shivered, and he didn't think before wrapping his arm around her, pulling her into his side.

"For warmth," she said, but her voice shook.

"For warmth," he agreed, though warmth was suddenly the least of his problems. His whole body had gone hyperaware—heart hammering, skin too sensitive even through layers of clothing, every nerve ending focused on the places where they touched.

She fit against him perfectly, her head finding the dip below his shoulder like it had been designed for her. This close, vanilla mixed with chocolate and the clean scent of snow. Her hand rested on his knee, casual except for the way her thumb moved in small circles that were definitely not casual at all. Each rotation sent heat spiraling up his thigh, making it hard to remember how to breathe normally.

"Tell me about San Francisco," she said quietly.

The question snapped him fully out of his spiral of want. "What about it?"

"The job. Your aunt mentioned it."

He tensed, and she must have felt it because her hand squeezed his knee gently. The lighthouse beam washed over them, illuminating her face tilted up toward his, patient and open.

"Deputy Chief of Emergency Medicine at SF General," he said finally. "Dr. Whitmore is retiring, and the current deputy, even when she becomes chief, will probably retire in a few years. My mother has... connections."

"It's a good opportunity?"

"It's everything she planned. Everything I'm supposed to want." The words tasted bitter compared to the lingering sweetness of chocolate. "Prestige, advancement, research opportunities."

"But?"

He looked down at her, at the way snow had settled on her dark hair like a crown, at the understanding in her eyes. "But it's not here."

The words hung between them, heavy with implication. Her thumb had stopped moving on his knee.

"I have something to tell you too," she said. "The lighthouse project ends in February. I already have potential offers—Maritime Museum in Maine, another preservation project in Washington state."

"Good opportunities?"

She smiled sadly. "I'm good at leaving, remember?"

"What if you weren't?"

The question surprised them both. Kelsey sat up slightly, turning to face him more fully, and the loss of her warmth against his side was almost painful.

"I don't know how to not leave," she admitted. "It's what I do. Document and go. Before things get complicated."

"Things are already complicated."

"I know." She was biting her lip again, and his resolve cracked.

"I should tell you something," he said.

"What?"

"I haven't stopped thinking about kissing you."

Her breath caught, visible in the cold air between them. "Since October?"

"Since the library. Since this morning. Since you walked into breakfast in October and looked like you wanted to fight the coffee maker." He reached up, gloved thumb brushing her lower lip. "Since you bit your lip just like this."

"Marcus." Just his name, but weighted with everything.

Her hand came up to his face, leather against his cold cheek. "I bite my lip when I'm nervous."

"I know."

"I'm not nervous now."

The world narrowed to just them—the snow falling like blessings, the lighthouse sweeping them in silver, the sighs of the lake against the shore. He leaned in slowly, giving her time to pull away.

Instead she met him halfway.

The first touch was soft, careful, a question asked and answered. Her lips were cold at first, tasting of chocolate and promise. Then she made a soft sound against his mouth, her hand sliding into his hair, and careful went out the window.

He pulled her closer, one hand tangling in her hair while the other spanned her back, feeling the way she trembled against him. She opened for him, and the kiss deepened into something desperate and necessary. When her tongue touched his, his whole world tilted. This wasn't like October's first kiss against the lighthouse—shock, wonder, jump away, embarrassment. This was deeper, surer, like coming home and jumping off a cliff at the same time.

The lighthouse beam swept over them, and he could see the golden light through his closed eyelids, or maybe that was just what kissing Kelsey felt like—like being illuminated from the inside, like every cell in his body was suddenly, brilliantly alive.

They broke apart only when oxygen became necessary, both breathing hard in the cold air, breaths mingling in visible clouds between them. He rested his forehead against hers, unwilling to give up contact entirely. His heart was trying to beat its way out of his chest, and he could feel her pulse racing where his hand curved around her neck.

"God, Marcus," she breathed against his mouth. "You can't—we can't—"

"I know." But he kissed her again anyway, softer this time but no less intense, trying to memorize everything

—the way she sighed into his mouth, how perfectly she fit against him, the little catch in her breath when he kissed the corner of her jaw.

His phone buzzed in his pocket. Then again. They broke apart reluctantly, and he fumbled for it with clumsy fingers, every nerve ending still focused on her.

"It's my mother," he said, seeing the caller ID.

"Answer it?"

"Not a chance." He declined the call, but reality had crept back in. Kelsey's phone was lighting up too.

She laughed shakily, still pressed against him. "Katie wants to know how stargazing is going. In all caps. With about seventeen question marks."

"Tell her we saw stars," he said, which made her laugh out loud. He felt the vibration of it everywhere they touched.

But the spell was shifting. The snow was starting to fall, and even with body heat and hot chocolate, the December cold was winning. Though with Kelsey still close, still touching him, he could barely feel it.

"What happens now?" she asked quietly, her fingers playing with the hair at the nape of his neck, sending shivers down his spine.

"I don't know." He was honest because she deserved that. "I just know I want—"

"What?"

"Time. With you. To figure this out." He cupped

her face, thumb stroking her cheekbone, feeling her lean into the touch. "To see if what I think this could be is actually what it could be."

"I want that too." She leaned into his touch. "I'm scared."

"Me too."

"Okay. As long as we're scared together."

He kissed her again, quick, sweet and soft this time, tasting promise more than passion. The lighthouse beam found them one more time, blessing or warning, he couldn't tell.

"We should go back," she said reluctantly, pressing one more kiss to his mouth like she couldn't help herself. "Before we freeze to the log."

"Or before Katie sends a search party."

They packed up slowly, neither wanting the night to end.

When they stood, he took her hand properly, interlacing their fingers even through gloves.

The walk back was different—closer, warmer despite the snow.

They stopped just in the shadow of the porch, not quite ready to face their audience.

"Thank you," she said.

"For what?"

"For being worth driving through a snowstorm for."

He kissed her again because he had to, because she

was standing there in the snow looking at him like he was something wonderful instead of a burned-out resident who didn't know what he wanted beyond this moment, this woman, this place that felt like home.

The inn's front door was like a stage entrance. They could see their audience through the windows—Beatrice with her knitting, Cordelia sweeping a pristine floor, Katie practically vibrating with curiosity.

"Ready?" he asked.

"No. Yes. Maybe." She squeezed his hand. "Together?"

"Together."

They walked in to warmth and light and absolutely no subtlety whatsoever.

"Productive stargazing?" Agnes asked without looking up from her knitting.

Marcus felt heat flood his face. Beside him, Kelsey made a sound that might have been a laugh or a whimper.

"Very educational," Kelsey managed. "We saw... constellations."

"I'll bet you did," Katie said gleefully. "Is that why your lips are all—"

"Lovely, dears," Beatrice interrupted.

They escaping up the staircase. But in the hallway, away from eyes, Marcus couldn't help pulling her close again. Running his hand down her hair, freshly tousled from her red knit cap.

"Breakfast tomorrow?" he asked.

"It's a date." She paused. "Our third? Fourth?"

"Who's counting?"

He kissed her once more, pressing her back against her door, feeling her arch into him. For a moment, he thought about asking to come in, about continuing this somewhere warm and private. The way she was looking at him, pupils dark and wide, lips swollen from his kisses, he thought she might say yes.

"Marcus," she breathed, and he heard the want in it, the same desperate need he felt.

"I know. I should go." But he kissed her again, deeper, his hands framing her face.

"You really should." Another kiss.

"Going now." One more.

Finally, she pushed gently at his chest, laughing shakily. "Goodnight, Marcus."

"Goodnight."

He made himself walk away, though every step felt wrong. At his own door, he looked back to find her still watching, leaning against her doorframe like her knees were weak.

"Go inside before I come back over there," he said.

She smiled, slow and devastating. "Threat? Or promise?"

"Kelsey." Her name came out like a plea.

"Going, going." She disappeared into her room.

Marcus floated into his room, lips still tingling, the taste of her lingering like a promise. His whole body hummed with want, skin too sensitive, heart still racing. Outside his window, the lighthouse had gone dark again, its job apparently done for the night.

But Marcus lay awake for hours, reliving every moment—the crunch of snow, the warmth of her against his side, the way she'd said his name like it was the only word that mattered. The smell of her hair, the sound of her laugh, the feel of her hands in his hair. The way she'd kissed him like she was drowning and he was air.

Tomorrow there would be a wedding. Tomorrow there would be questions about San Francisco and lighthouse projects and what happened when February came.

But tonight—tonight he'd kissed Kelsey Winters under stars and snow until neither of them could breathe, and the world had shifted into something new and terrifying and absolutely worth the risk.

Tonight, that was enough.

Chapter Ten

Kelsey woke up late, and happy. She scootched up in bed, watching big snowflakes fall past her window reliving every second of last night in vivid, heart-racing detail. Her lips still felt swollen, sensitive when she touched them. She could still taste him—chocolate and winter and that indefinable something that was just Marcus. Her whole body hummed like a tuning fork that had been struck and couldn't stop vibrating.

Every time she closed her eyes, she was back on that beach, his hands in her hair, his mouth hot and desperate against hers. The way he'd groaned when she'd nipped his lower lip. The way he'd pressed her against her door like he was trying to memorize the shape of her.

The lighthouse book lay open on her nightstand to a page about "guiding lights home," though she didn't remember turning to it.

Her camera sat untouched on the dresser. For the first time in years, she didn't want a lens between her and the memory. Didn't want to reduce last night to pixels and composition. She wanted it raw and real and entirely hers. The scratch of bark through the blanket, the heat of his mouth. The shiver it was calling up right now.

Her phone buzzed on the nightstand.

Good morning

Two words from Marcus, and her heart did a complicated flip. She typed back with fingers that trembled slightly.

Good morning, you

Three dots appeared immediately, and she bit her lip waiting for his response.

Breakfast in 20? Before the chaos?

The flutter in her stomach intensified. She'd see him in twenty minutes. After last night. After kisses that had rewired her entire nervous system. How was she supposed to sit across from him and eat breakfast like her whole world hadn't tilted off its axis?

How could she not?

Yes

She dressed carefully—jeans and a soft green sweater

that brought out her eyes. Not that she was trying to look good. Not that she'd changed sweaters twice. Her hands shook as she applied lip gloss, remembering his mouth on hers, his hands in her hair, the sounds he'd made when she'd—

"Stop it," she told her reflection firmly.

As if.

The inn was quiet as she made her way downstairs, that particular pre-wedding hush of a building holding its breath. But the kitchen was already alive with warmth and the smell of cinnamon rolls. Beatrice was pulling something that smelled sweet and good from an oven.

Agnes stood in front of the big kitchen table, which was covered in what looked to be three complete sets of tableware.

"Coffee's fresh," she said. "Everybody in the dining room today. No space in here."

Kelsey pushed through the swinging door to find Marcus at her usual corner table, already nursing coffee and wearing a white button-down that made his skin glow in the morning light. When he looked up and saw her, his face softened into something private and warm.

"Morning," she said, unable to stop her answering smile.

"Morning." He pulled out the chair beside him instead of letting her sit across. "Sleep well?"

The question was innocent enough, but the way his

fingers brushed hers as she sat—deliberate, familiar—made heat pool in her stomach. "Eventually."

His thumb traced a small circle on her wrist before Agnes appeared with loaded plates.

"Eat," Agnes commanded, but her stern expression cracked slightly when she saw their joined hands on the table. "Both of you. Long day ahead."

As Agnes retreated, Marcus shifted closer, his thigh pressing against hers under the table. It was such a simple touch, but the casual intimacy of it—the assumption that they could just be close now—made her chest tight with something beyond desire.

"You're wearing the blue sweater," he observed, voice low enough that only she could hear. "The one that matches your eyes when you're happy."

She turned to look at him, surprised. "You noticed my sweater?"

"I notice everything about you." He said it simply, like a fact, while cutting into his pancakes. "Have since October."

Before she could respond, Beatrice burst through the door in a whirlwind of flour and excitement.

"Oh, there you are! Both of you!" She stopped short, taking in how close they were sitting, the easy way Marcus's hand rested on Kelsey's chair back. "Well, don't you two look cozy this morning. Beautiful night for stargazing, wasn't it?"

"Beautiful," Kelsey agreed, meeting Marcus's eyes. He smiled—that new smile she'd discovered last night, the one that was just for her.

"The lighthouse was on for hours," Beatrice continued, clearly fishing. "Harold Weatherby called to complain, but I told him some lights are worth celebrating."

Marcus's fingers found the nape of Kelsey's neck, a light touch that made her shiver. "Some definitely are."

Beatrice clasped her hands together, beaming. "Oh, I'm so glad you two figured things out. Agnes owes me twenty dollars. I said you'd sort it before the wedding, and she said—"

"Beatrice," Agnes called from the kitchen. "The flowers are here."

"Coming!" But she paused at the door, smile going soft. "You two remind me of Robert and Margaret when they were young. Same way of looking at each other like the rest of the world's just background noise."

After she left, they ate in comfortable quiet, bodies angled toward each other. Marcus stole bites of her fruit; she claimed half his toast. Normal couple things that felt revolutionary after years of careful distance from everyone.

"Nervous about the photos?" he asked, refilling her coffee without being asked—he'd already learned she liked it stronger than the inn usually made it.

"No." She considered. "Well, maybe about not crying during the ceremony. Weddings didn't used to get to me, but now…"

"Now you know what it feels like," he finished. "To want that. With someone specific."

She looked at him, this man who'd driven through a snowstorm for her, who'd shown her his childhood fears and his adult ones, who touched her like she was precious but kissed her like she was necessary.

"Yeah," she said softly. "Now I know."

His hand covered hers on the table, and she turned her palm up to interlace their fingers. Such a simple gesture, but Agnes made a satisfied sound from the doorway.

"Good," the older woman said. "You figured out how to sit together without combusting. Progress." But her eyes were warm. "Kelsey, Ella's waiting in the turret suite."

They stood reluctantly. In the doorway, Marcus caught her hand, tugging her close enough that she could smell his soap and the faint scent of her own perfume on his collar.

"Later?" he murmured against her ear. "After all the formal pictures?"

"Later," she promised, then surprised herself by rising on her toes to kiss him quickly—a casual goodbye kiss like they'd been doing this for years instead of hours.

His eyes went dark, but his smile was pure happiness. "Go make Ella beautiful."

She left him there, heading for the turret stairs, but she could feel his gaze following her. Could feel the invisible thread between them, new and strong and getting stronger with every passing hour.

Normal. They were learning to be normal together.

The thought made her grin all the way up the stairs.

The turret suite was already a hive of activity when Kelsey arrived, but stepping into the circular space stopped her breath completely. She'd been in plenty of hotel rooms, plenty of beautiful spaces, but this—this was something else entirely.

The room curved around her like being inside a jewelry box, all warm honey-colored walls and tall windows that wrapped around the space in an embrace of light. December's faded morning light poured through the glass in streams of silver, and every surface seemed to catch and amplify it—the brass fixtures gleaming like captured sunshine, the hardwood floors polished to a mirror shine that reflected the ceiling's gentle curves.

The scent hit her next, layering over her senses like a complex perfume: Sarah's lavender sachets tucked everywhere, the vanilla-and-roses sweetness of wedding flowers scattered across surfaces, and underneath it all, the indefinable smell of old wood that had absorbed decades of love and laughter and tears. Coffee drifted up from somewhere below, mixing with the sharper scent of hairspray and the warm musk of excited women in close quarters.

Katie was trying to untangle pantyhose with manic energy near the curved bench by a bank of windows, muttering what sounded like extremely creative profanity under her breath. Mrs. Frankl stood beside the antique dressing table—mahogany with a three-way mirror that caught light like a kaleidoscope—using a hand steamer to press invisible wrinkles from something draped across her arm with the focused intensity of a surgeon. And Ella stood in the center of it all in a silk robe the color of champagne, her dark hair already twisted into an elegant updo that made her neck look swan-like, looking radiant and only slightly panicked.

The circular space made everything feel intimate, conspiratorial, like they were all part of some ancient ritual. Which, Kelsey supposed, they were.

"Thank heavens," Ella said when she saw Kelsey, relief flooding her voice. "I need documentation that I didn't completely lose my mind this morning."

Kelsey raised her camera instinctively, but found

herself still cataloguing the room through her photographer's eye. The way the morning light created patterns on the curved walls; how it would change during the day. The comfortable chaos of wedding preparation—makeup scattered across the dressing table, shoes kicked off near the four-poster bed that dominated one side of the space, ribbons and pins and the detritus of getting ready spread across every surface like confetti.

"You look beautiful," Kelsey assured her, adjusting her camera settings for the tricky circular light. "What's wrong?"

"Nothing. Everything. I'm getting married in less than an hour and I can't remember how to breathe and —" Ella stopped, studying Kelsey's face with the laser focus of someone who'd learned to read people's stories. "No. Way."

"What?" Kelsey's finger froze on the shutter release.

"You kissed him."

Kelsey nearly dropped her camera, the weight of it suddenly awkward in hands that had gone clumsy. "How does everyone—"

"You look different. Softer. Like butter that's been left in the sun." Ella's grin was radiant, transforming her whole face. "Also, you're glowing. And you keep touching your lips."

Heat flooded Kelsey's cheeks as she snatched her

hand away from her mouth. The circular room seemed to amplify her embarrassment, bouncing it back at her from every curved wall. "I'm not glowing."

"You're totally glowing," Katie said, abandoning the pantyhose to turn and stare. Her sandy hair was already perfectly arranged; her bridesmaid's dress a deep forest green that brought out her eyes. "And you look thoroughly kissed. Like, extremely thoroughly. Still. Tell us everything. Was it romantic? Was it under the stars? Did the lighthouse—"

"The dress!" Mrs. Frankl interrupted firmly, but Kelsey caught the amused sparkle in her eyes. "Perhaps we should focus on the dress?"

She moved to the tall armoire that stood between two windows, its dark wood almost black with age. When she unzipped a garment bag with reverent hands, the sound seemed amplified in the space. Kelsey hold her breath.

The dress that emerged made everyone in the room gasp.

Through her viewfinder, Kelsey watched vintage lace unfold like magic. The color of winter moonlight, it seemed to capture every ray of the light nearby, making the fabric almost luminescent. Long sleeves that would hug Ella's arms, a neckline that was modest and elegant, and tiny pearl buttons that marched up the back like soldiers in formation. The skirt fell in gentle folds that would move like water when Ella walked.

But it was more than just fabric and design. Looking at the dress, Kelsey could feel its history. The love it had witnessed, the joy it had celebrated, the decades it had waited in patient darkness for exactly this moment.

"It was Sarah's," Mrs. Frankl said softly, her voice thick with emotion. "From her wedding in 1952. She kept it all these years, stored perfectly, as if..."

"As if she was waiting," Ella finished, eyes filling with tears. "Oh. It's perfect."

The scent of preservation lavender rose from the fabric as Mrs. Frankl laid it carefully across the bed, and Kelsey framed the shot she found herself thinking about time, about love that transcended years, about the way some things were meant to last.

As they helped Ella into the dress—Katie managing the dozens of tiny buttons with surprisingly patient fingers, Mrs. Frankl adjusting lace with the precise touch of someone who understood fabric and fit, Kelsey documenting every moment through her lens—the turret suite filled with a warmth that had nothing to do with the heating system.

The room seemed to hum with contentment, its light shifting and dancing across the curved walls as if the space itself was celebrating. Through her viewfinder, she captured Ella's face as the dress settled around her—

wonder and joy and something deeper, something that looked like coming home. The lace seemed to transform her, making her not just beautiful but luminous, like she was lit from within.

Patricia Thompson appeared in the doorway just as Mrs. Frankl fastened the last button, and the temperature in the room shifted. Not colder, exactly, but charged, like the moment before a storm breaks.

"Ella?" Her voice was uncertain. "May I come in?"

The circular room went still, as if even the inn itself was holding its breath. Ella turned, the dress rustling softly around her, and for a moment mother and daughter just looked at each other across the space that suddenly felt both vast and intimate.

Kelsey raised her camera slowly, gently, knowing this was the kind of moment that could shatter if handled wrong. Through the lens, she saw two women seeing each other—really seeing each other—for the first time in years.

"Mom," Ella said softly, the word carrying more emotion than seemed possible in one syllable. "Of course."

The scent of Patricia's perfume—something expensive and floral—mixed with the room's existing aromatherapy of lavender and roses and old wood, creating a complex bouquet that spoke of past and present colliding. Kelsey captured the moment Patricia stepped forward and Ella met her halfway, the vintage lace catching light as she moved.

"You look beautiful," Patricia whispered, her voice breaking slightly. "Just like—"

"Like Grandma," Ella finished, and her smile was radiant enough to power the whole inn. "I know. I feel her here."

And in that moment, in the golden light of the turret suite with the scent of lavender and love filling the air, Kelsey felt it too—Sarah's presence, warm and approving, as if the inn itself was blessing this reunion.

"She'd be so proud." Patricia touched the lace gently, reverently, and Kelsey caught the gesture through her lens. "She always said you'd come back. Said the inn would call you home when you were ready."

Katie sniffled loudly from her position by the windows, and when Kelsey turned her camera toward her, she saw the younger woman wiping her eyes with the back of her hand, mascara slightly smudged but still beautiful.

"Okay, everyone stop being emotional or my mascara will run and Liam will think I've been crying over his wedding."

That broke the tension like a soap bubble popping, and soon they were all laughing, the sound bouncing off the curved walls and filling the space with joy. The turret suite returned to controlled chaos—finishing preparations with the easy camaraderie of women preparing for battle. Or in this case, for love.

The light had shifted as they worked, and now it poured through the windows in streams of pure gold, making Ella's dress shimmer like captured starlight. Mrs. Frankl fussed with the final adjustments, her fingers sure and gentle on the vintage fabric. Katie reapplied her mascara with the precision of someone who'd perfected the art of wedding-day touch-ups. Patricia fiddled with the simple headband that held a short veil.

"Ella's hair never takes well to confinement," she said, grimly determined as if she was going to change all that today.

Downstairs, the inn was buzzing with final preparations when she returned. The parlor had been transformed beyond even yesterday's beauty—candles everywhere, white roses and evergreen creating an enchanted forest feel.

"Beautiful things happen when people choose love over fear," Agnes said pointedly. "The inn knows that. Sarah knew that. Question is, do you?"

Before Kelsey could respond, Agnes was gone, leaving only the lingering scent of cardamom.

Then she saw Marcus.

Katie hadn't been exaggerating. In his full suit, he was devastating. The charcoal gray made his skin glow, the jacket emphasized his broad shoulders, and the formal lines made him look like every romantic hero she'd ever imagined.

But it was more than that. It was the way he carried himself, the quiet confidence mixed with the vulnerability she'd seen at the beach. The way his hands—those hands that had been in her hair last night—now adjusted Liam's boutonniere with gentle precision.

He must have felt her looking because he turned, their eyes meeting across the parlor. The heat in his gaze made her hands shake so badly she nearly dropped her camera. How was she supposed to photograph a wedding when all she could think about was the promise in his eyes? Everything. He wanted everything.

"Places, everyone!" Robert called. "Sit, sit. Let's get a move on."

Marcus sat at the end the middle row on the left, an empty space on his left waiting for his aunt. Agnes, Beatrice, and an already teary Cordelia sat to his right. Outside of them and the Carter relatives, it looked like the rest of the townspeople didn't pick a side, just filled in.

And the room was full.

Kelsey took her position, camera ready.

Mrs. Frankl began to play Canon in D on the violin,

the notes floating through the space like blessings. The doors opened, and the wedding party began to enter.

And as Ella appeared in the doorway, radiant in Sarah's dress with light streaming around her like magic made visible, Kelsey raised her camera and prepared to document love.

Chapter Eleven

Marcus tried to concentrate on the words and the people in front of him. Robert Carter had worked so hard on this ceremony—even to the point of getting himself elected mayor last month so he could officiate, to hear Katie tell the story.

Liam glowed. His brother Tom, who'd actually made it with twenty minutes to spare, stood beside him. Blond like his brother, and burly, he looked like he'd run all the way here from DC, red and still trying to catch his breath.

The parlor had transformed into something from a fairy tale.

But all he could see was Kelsey.

She moved through the space like water, camera

raised, capturing moments with the same intensity she'd kissed him on the beach last night. Every time she bent for a different angle, every time she brushed her hair behind her ear, every time she bit that damn lip while adjusting her settings, his body responded like she was touching him.

Like last night. The memory made his skin feel too tight, his formal clothes too restrictive.

Everything.

He'd told her he wanted everything.

The word sat in his chest like a lit fuse.

His phone vibrated in his pocket. His mother again, the third call today. He'd sent her to voicemail each time, but her persistence was legendary. She wanted an answer about San Francisco. Wanted to know why he was "wasting time at some provincial wedding" when he should be preparing for his interview.

Should've left the phone upstairs.

Aunt Mei-Lin began to play. The opening notes of Canon in D filled the space, and the assembled guests rose to their feet and turned toward the parlor doors. The doors opened, and Katie appeared in deep green silk that complemented her coloring perfectly.

She walked with the particular confidence of someone who knew she looked good, but when she caught Marcus's eye, her wink was pure mischief.

Then the atmosphere in the room changed. Ella must be here.

Everyone faced the doors, but Marcus found himself watching Liam instead.

His friend's whole face transformed the moment Ella appeared. All the nervousness, all the fidgeting, all of it melted away into pure wonder. It was like watching someone recognize their home after being lost. Relief and joy and absolute certainty all at once.

Marcus turned to see what had caused that transformation, and his breath caught.

Ella floated down the aisle in Sarah's dress, the vintage lace seeming to capture and hold light. She looked like something from another era, timeless and ethereal, but it was her expression that made Marcus's chest tight. She looked at Liam like he was her whole world, like everything that had come before had just been the path leading to this moment.

Marcus looked for Kelsey, found her in the corner next to Tom, her camera to her face, tears tracking down her cheeks. But she was smiling.

"Dearly beloved," Robert Carter began, his voice carrying easily, "we gather today in this place of magic and healing to witness the union of two hearts that have found their home in each other."

The words hit Marcus like a punch to the chest. Home. Was that what this feeling was? This desperate need to be wherever Kelsey was, to wake up to her camera clicking and fall asleep to her quiet breathing? This feeling like his skin didn't fit right when she wasn't near?

Robert continued, speaking about choice and commitment, about building something beautiful in a beautiful place, about love that transforms everything it touches. Marcus found himself hanging on every word, imagining them being said to him, by him, about them. His eyes kept finding Kelsey, watching the way she moved, the grace in her movements.

"Liam," Robert said, "your vows."

Liam took Ella's hands, and his voice was steady. "Ella Thompson, three months ago, you stood in this inn's kitchen, ready to fight the universe for a cup of coffee. That's when I knew you were the bravest person I'd ever met."

Soft laughter rippled through the room.

"You chose magic over money, wonder over safety, love over fear," Liam continued. "You saw what this place could be and fought for it when everyone else said you were crazy. You made me believe again, made me remember that some things are worth choosing even when you can't explain why."

Marcus's throat went tight. Kelsey's hands in his hair, her body pressed against his, her voice when she said his name.

"I choose you, Ella Thompson," Liam said, voice strong with certainty. "I choose to be your guardian, your partner, your anchor when the magic gets overwhelming and your believer when the world says we're both insane. I choose to love you in this life and whatever comes after, to tend this magic with you, to build something beautiful in this place that brought us together."

Ella was crying openly now, but her smile could have powered the inn. When she spoke, her voice carried the same certainty, but Marcus barely heard the words. Kelsey had moved for a better angle, putting her directly in his line of sight. The winter light streaming through the windows backlit her, making her glow.

"—home isn't a place you're born into—it's a place you choose to build with someone who sees your heart and decides it's worth protecting," Ella continued.

The words penetrated his fog, and Marcus sucked in a breath. He looked at Kelsey again, catching every moment, and thought about building. About choosing. About San Francisco and lighthouse projects and how none of it mattered as much as the way she made him feel whole.

"The rings," Robert prompted gently.

Tom produced them smoothly, and as Liam slid the white-gold band onto Ella's finger, the sand globe in the lobby chimed—a clear, bell-like sound that seemed to come from everywhere and nowhere. Several guests gasped, looking around for the source.

"By the power vested in me," Robert said, his voice seeming to come from very far away, "and by the love that fills this room and this inn and this community that claims you both, I pronounce you husband and wife."

The lighthouse beam swept across the windows, brilliant despite the midday sun. This time, everyone saw it, and the gasp was collective. But Marcus barely noticed, too focused on the way Kelsey's thumb had brushed across his knuckles before she pulled away.

"You may kiss your bride," Robert added unnecessarily, because Liam was already cupping Ella's face, already leaning in.

The kiss was perfect—tender and certain and full of promise. Around them, rose petals began to fall from nowhere, drifting down like snow despite the closed room. The inn's opinion, made visible.

The room erupted in cheers and applause. Ella and Liam broke apart, laughing and crying, faces bright with joy. The new couple didn't bother going back down the tiny aisle. They just started hugging the first person they saw in the front row and carried on until they'd shared their love with everyone in the room.

His aunt appeared before him, elegant in burgundy silk, her expression knowing.

"Your mother called me," she said without preamble. "Three times."

"Aunt Mei-Lin—"

"She's concerned about your interview. Apparently, you haven't confirmed your flight." Her gaze drifted to where Kelsey was directing a group photo, then back to him. "Though I'm beginning to understand why."

Behind her, he could see Kelsey laughing at something Katie said, the sound carrying through the windows and straight to his chest. She'd tucked a strand of hair behind her ear, and he wanted to trace that path with his fingers, his mouth—

"Marcus," his aunt said gently. "You're staring."

Heat flooded his face. "I'm not—"

"You are. Like a man dying of thirst watching water." She studied him with those eyes that missed nothing. "What will you choose, nephew?"

His phone buzzed again. This time, when he looked, it was a text from his mother: *Board wants answer by Monday. Stop being childish*

"I don't know," he said, but even as the words left his mouth, he knew they were a lie.

"Yes," Mei-Lin said gently, "you do. You've known since October. The question is whether you're brave enough to disappoint Helena Chen."

During a break while Kelsey changed lenses, she moved closer, and he could smell her vanilla scent mixed with the cold winter air. His hands clenched with the effort of not reaching for her.

"You okay?" she asked quietly.

"No," he said honestly. "We can talk about it later."

Her breath caught, and color flooded her cheeks. "Marcus—"

"Such a beautiful wedding," he said. "They'll be so glad you were here to capture it all."

The transformation of the parlor happened with the efficiency of a well-rehearsed dance. Townspeople helped move chairs and shift furniture, and suddenly the ceremony space became a reception hall. Marcus himself move all the chairs, needing the physical activity to burn off some of the tension coiled in his muscles.

"Ladies and gentlemen," Robert announced, "please join me in welcoming, for the first time, Mr. and Mrs. Liam Thompson Carter!"

Ella and Liam entered to thunderous applause, both glowing with the particular light of perfect happiness. The opening notes of "At Last" began again, and they moved to the small dance floor that had been cleared near the fireplace.

She stood across the room now, camera lowered, just

watching the dance with soft eyes. The afternoon light through the windows caught her profile, and he was moving before he thought better of it.

"Dance with me?"

The words came out rougher than intended, more demand than question. She looked up, and the heat in her eyes nearly knocked him back.

"I'm working," she said, but her protest was breathless.

"One dance." He held out his hand, watched her eye it like it might bite. "Please, Kelsey. I need—"

He stopped, but she heard what he didn't say. *I need to touch you. I need to hold you. I need to pretend for three minutes that you're mine.*

She set her camera carefully on a table and let him lead her onto the floor. The moment his hand found her waist, the moment she stepped into his arms, his whole body sighed in relief. Then she pressed closer, and relief turned to torture.

"Hi," she said softly, and he could feel her breath against his neck.

"Hi."

They swayed together, finding their rhythm, and Marcus let himself imagine this was their wedding. Their first dance. Their beginning. Her hand on his shoulder burned through his jacket, and where their other hands clasped, he could feel her pulse racing to match his.

"Your aunt looked serious earlier," Kelsey observed, but her voice was breathy, distracted.

"My mother's applying pressure. About San Francisco."

She tensed in his arms, and he pulled her closer instinctively. "When do you have to decide?"

"Sunday, apparently. Interview's Monday."

"So soon."

"Yes." He gave in to temptation and pressed his face against her hair, breathing her in. "But not as soon as tonight."

She shivered against him, and when she looked up, her eyes were dark with the same desperate want he felt. "No," she agreed. "Not as soon as tonight."

The song was ending, other music beginning, but they kept dancing. Around them, the reception continued—laughter and champagne and joy—but Marcus only had eyes for the woman in his arms who was trembling against him.

"Marcus," she said quietly. "What are we doing?"

"Dancing," he said, though they both knew she meant more than that.

"You know what I mean."

He did. What were they doing, starting something when February loomed? When San Francisco called?

When she had lighthouses to photograph in distant states?

"I don't know," he admitted. "I just know I don't want to stop."

"Neither do I," she whispered, and the admission seemed to surprise her. "That terrifies me."

"Me too."

"Good." She smiled, small but real. "As long as we're terrified together."

The echo of her words from last night made him pull her impossibly closer, and they danced through another song, lost in their own world of barely restrained want and growing certainty.

Finally, duty called—Kelsey needed to photograph the cake cutting, Marcus was pulled into a toast—but the promise of tonight hummed between them like a live wire.

As he watched her work, capturing joy and love with hands that still trembled slightly, Marcus made a decision. Monday could bring whatever it would bring. San Francisco could wait. His mother could rage.

Tonight, he was going to choose courage.

Tonight, he was going to choose Kelsey.

Tonight, he was going to choose home.

And from the way she kept looking at him—heat and promise and barely leashed want—she was going to choose him too.

Chapter Twelve

Kelsey floated through the next hour of the reception in a haze of sense memory and anticipation. Her body still hummed from dancing with Marcus, every nerve ending alive with the phantom pressure of his hands. She tried to focus on her work—photographing speeches, capturing candid moments of joy—but her awareness kept drifting to him across the room. Every time their eyes met, heat flashed between them like summer lightning.

Tonight. The promise of it thrummed through her bloodstream.

She was framing a shot of Ella laughing at something Tom had said in his best man speech when her phone buzzed in her pocket. She ignored it—unprofessional to check phones during speeches. But it buzzed again. And again.

The third time, she glanced at the screen. Richard Lawson, Maine Maritime Museum. Her contact for the lighthouse preservation project. Why was he calling on a Friday afternoon?

The phone stopped, then immediately started again.

"—and that's when I knew Liam was completely gone for her, even from seven hundred miles away," Tom was saying to general laughter. Kelsey captured the moment, then slipped quietly toward the lobby. Whatever Richard wanted, it must be urgent.

"Kelsey! Thank God," Richard's voice boomed the moment she answered. "I've been trying to reach you all day."

"I'm at a wedding, Richard. Working." She kept her voice low, moving further from the parlor doors. "What's so urgent?"

"The board met yesterday. Emergency session." He paused for dramatic effect—Richard loved his dramatic pauses. "They've approved the new position. Director of Lighthouse Documentation. Leading a team of three photographers, full benefits, and Kelsey—the salary."

He named a figure that made her lean against the wall for support.

"That's..." She couldn't finish. It was more than

double what she made now, cobbling together freelance projects.

"I know. And there's more. Two-year minimum contract with an option to extend. We'll provide housing—there's a beautiful apartment in the Old Port district. Full relocation assistance."

Her mind spun. This was it—the recognition she'd worked for, the chance to lead rather than just document. She could easily stay in one place for two years.

Everything she'd thought she wanted. She wouldn't be "the photographer from October" anymore. She'd be Kelsey Winters, Director. Someone with a title, a team, a future that made sense on paper.

Marcus's face flashed in her mind. His eyes when he'd said he wanted everything.

"When?" she managed.

"That's the thing. We need you to start January 15th. I know it's fast, but we've got the Pemaquid Point project scheduled for February, and you're the only one who knows that lighthouse well enough to lead it. If you can get here for that, we can rejigger schedules so you can close out your other assignments."

January 15th. Four weeks. The walls of the lobby seemed to close in. She dropped to a seat on the bottom step of the wide staircase.

"Kelsey? You still there?"

"Yes, sorry. I'm just... processing."

"I know it's a lot to take in. But here's the thing—the board wants an answer by Tuesday. They have another candidate, but I've pushed hard for you. You're the best, Kelsey. This project needs you."

Tuesday. Three days.

"Can I... can I call you back? I need to think."

"Of course! But don't think too long. This is your chance, Kelsey. The kind of opportunity that doesn't come twice."

She ended the call and sat in the empty lobby, phone clutched in her hand. Through the parlor doors, she could hear laughter, music, joy. The sounds of people choosing love and permanence and roots.

Four weeks.

Tuesday deadline.

Everything she'd worked for.

She pressed her fingers to her lips, remembering Marcus's mouth there last night. Remembering his spikey teenage hair. Remembering everything.

"Get it together," she whispered to herself. She had a wedding to photograph. She could process this later. Talk to Marcus tonight. Figure out what any of this meant.

She plastered on her professional smile and slipped back into the reception.

The parlor was warm with laughter and champagne toasts. Kelsey tried to lose herself in the work, and her hands were steady. But every shot felt like it was happening at a distance, like she was documenting someone else's life while hers tilted off its axis.

Four weeks. January 15th. Tuesday deadline.

She was adjusting her settings for twilight when the reception energy suddenly shifted. Conversations quieted, then resumed at a different pitch. She looked up from her camera to see people stepping aside near the entrance, creating a path for someone who clearly expected it.

The tiny woman was elegant in the way that came from money and breeding and absolute certainty of her place in the world. Her black suit was severely cut but obviously expensive, her silver hair arranged in a perfect chignon. She moved through the reception like a blade, cutting through the warm chaos without being touched by it.

Kelsey knew who she was before anyone said a word. The cheekbones were the same, the careful way of moving, the assessing gaze that catalogued everything and found it wanting.

Dr. Helena Chen had arrived.

Across the room, Kelsey saw Mei-Lin's face go carefully neutral—the expression of someone preparing for battle. But it was Marcus's reaction that made her heart clench.

He'd been laughing at something Robert Carter

said, relaxed and happy in a way she'd rarely seen. The moment he spotted his mother, everything changed. His shoulders straightened, his smile became fixed, his whole body language shifted into something formal and distant. He looked younger suddenly, like a very tall boy caught doing something wrong.

Helena found him immediately, zeroing in with laser focus. The dutiful double kiss on the cheeks they exchanged had all the warmth of a business transaction.

Kelsey raised her camera instinctively—shield and defense and way to watch without being obvious. Through her viewfinder, she saw Helena's lips moving, Marcus nodding. Saw the way his jaw tightened, the way his hands clasped behind his back like he was at attention.

Then Helena's gaze swept the room and found her.

Even across the space, even with the bulky camera between them, that look was like being dissected. The older woman took in everything—Kelsey's professional but not designer clothes, her camera, her position documenting rather than participating.

In those few seconds, Kelsey felt herself weighed and dismissed.

Marcus must have said something because Helena's attention returned to him, but not before she said something that made his face go carefully blank. He glanced toward Kelsey, and she caught the apology in his eyes before someone moved between them, blocking her view.

"The photographer," she heard Helena say, the words carrying despite the distance. "From October."

Four words. That's all it took to reduce whatever they had to something small and dismissible.

The photographer. From October.

Not Kelsey. Not someone who mattered. Just a brief distraction from his real life.

Her phone buzzed. Richard again, texting this time: *Forgot to mention—the apartment has a darkroom. We can set you up with everything you need*

Everything she needed. As if that could be measured in square footage and equipment.

But maybe it could. Maybe being Kelsey Winters, Director, was better than being the photographer from October who'd foolishly thought eight days meant something.

She couldn't watch Marcus become someone else under his mother's influence. Couldn't stand here pretending to work while her future forked into two impossible paths. She needed air, space, somewhere to think.

Kelsey fled back to the lobby, relieved to find it still empty. Everyone was in the reception, celebrating love and forever while she tried to remember how to breathe. She ducked behind the massive welcome desk into the corner between the tall stool and the wall—a pocket of privacy where no one could see her from the main doors or hallway. She sank onto the floor, setting her camera carefully beside her.

The wood was solid beneath her, grounding. She pressed her hands against it, trying to find an anchor.

"There you are."

She looked up to find Katie squeezing into her space, concern written in her gaze. "I saw you bolt. Good hiding spot—I used to come here as a kid when I wanted to spy on guests."

"Nothing. I'm fine. Just taking a break."

"BS." Katie settled beside her on the floor, close in the confined space. "You look like someone just told you your dog died. Spill."

Kelsey opened her mouth to deflect again, but what came out was, "I got a job offer."

Katie shifted to face her better in the tight space. "Okay. That's good, right? Why do you look terrified?"

"Director position. Maine Maritime Museum. Leading the lighthouse documentation project." The words tumbled out like confession. "It's everything I've worked for. The salary is... it's life-changing money. Security I've never had."

"But?"

"But it starts January 15th." Kelsey's voice cracked. "Four weeks. They need an answer by Tuesday."

Katie was quiet for a moment, processing. Then, gently, "And?"

"Marcus." Kelsey laughed, but it came out broken. "Katie, Marcus and I have known each other eight days total. Eight days. What kind of person throws away a career opportunity for someone they've known eight days?"

"The kind who knows when something real is worth the risk?"

The words hit like cold water. "I'm not—we're not—it's too soon for that."

"Is it?" Katie studied her with those too-knowing eyes. "Because from where I'm sitting, you two look pretty gone for each other."

"His mother's here."

"I saw." Katie's expression darkened. "Hurricane Helena. She's already got him trapped in the dining room—didn't even stop for cake! Probably listing all the ways this wedding is beneath them."

"She looked at me like I was something stuck to her shoe."

"She looks at everyone like that. Even her sister, and she's a saint." Katie shifted in the cramped space. "But this isn't about Helena. This is about you and what you want."

"That's just it." Kelsey's hands clenched on her camera strap. "I don't know what I want. This job—it's safety, recognition, everything I've worked toward. I'd be Kelsey Winters, Director. Not just some freelance photographer. Someone with a real title, a real future. But Marcus..."

"Okay, but 'Kelsey Winters, Director' sounds like a Bond villain. Would you have to wear severe suits and say things like 'Execute Plan Lighthouse at dawn'?" She mimed an evil laugh, caught Kelsey's look of astonishment, and winced. "Sorry. Deflecting with humor. Carter family trait. But seriously—makes you want different things?"

"Makes me want to stay." The admission felt ripped from her chest. "And I don't know how to stay. I've never... I leave. It's what I do. Before it gets complicated, before it hurts, I leave."

They sat in their hidden corner for a moment, the sounds of the reception muffled but present. Past the stairs, Kelsey could see the open doors to the dining room. Could hear fragments of conversation drifting from the reception.

"—the San Francisco house has four bedrooms, perfect for when you start your family—"

"—Dr. McKhann's daughter just made partner at Whitman Sterling—"

"—really, Marcus, at your age you should be thinking about legacy—"

Helena's voice, carrying with the authority of

someone used to being obeyed. Each word carefully chosen to remind Marcus of the life she'd planned for him. The life that didn't include photographers from October who didn't even have permanent addresses.

"Maybe it's time to try something different," Katie said softly.

"Maybe." Kelsey picked up her camera, its weight familiar and comforting. "Or maybe his mother's right. Maybe I am just the photographer from October."

"You're more than that and you know it." Katie's voice went fierce. "I haven't seen Marcus happy like this since... ever, actually. He's been miserable for ten years, and then you show up and suddenly he's smiling again."

"For now. But what happens when the magic wears off? When he realizes we barely know each other? When he has to choose between me and the life he has planned?"

Katie looked like she wanted to argue more, but footsteps in the lobby stopped her. They both froze in their corner as Agnes's voice carried clearly.

"—saw her come this way. That girl needs to stop running and start staying."

The footsteps moved away, but Agnes's words lingered like prophecy.

"I should get back," Kelsey said finally. "Document the rest of the reception."

"Kelsey—"

"I need to think." She squeezed out of their hiding spot, Katie following. "And I need to work. It's what I'm here for, right? To document. Not to... whatever this is."

As she headed back toward the parlor, her mind kept spinning. Director of Lighthouse Documentation. A real salary. An apartment with a darkroom.

She paused at the parlor entrance, raising her camera to frame the scene. Through her viewfinder, she saw the whole story laid out. Ella and Liam, exhausted from dancing, flopped down on one of the velvet sofas that must have been rescued from its banishment on the porch. Guests drifting between them and the dining room, with the his and hers cakes and the open bar.

She drifted into the dining room, camera locked to her face. At a commandeered corner table,—their table—Marcus sat trapped while his mother gestured at her phone, probably showing him real estate listings or eligible doctors' daughters' LinkedIn profiles.

She focused her lens on the happy couple, but found herself pulling back, capturing the whole room instead. The way the light fell through the windows. The way strangers had become family for a day. The way Marcus sat imprisoned at his mother's table, his shoulders rigid with duty.

Documentary photography was about preserving what was, not what might be. She'd learned that long ago. Some stories you captured. Others you left before they could break your heart.

Her finger found the shutter.

Click.

Already a memory.

Four weeks. Eight days. Tuesday. The numbers spun in her head as she lowered her camera. She'd always been good at leaving. It was staying that terrified her.

Through the window, the lighthouse stood dark against the winter sky. Some lights, she thought, only showed you where you'd been. The question was whether that was enough to show you where to go.

Chapter Thirteen

Marcus had been laughing at Robert's story about Liam's first attempt at fixing a roof when the temperature in the room seemed to drop ten degrees. He didn't need to turn around to know why. After thirty-five years, he had a sixth sense for his mother's arrival—the way conversations quieted, the way people unconsciously straightened their posture, the way warmth fled from any space she entered.

Through the parlor windows, he watched the lighthouse beam sweep across the water and suddenly saw it as she would: a defunct structure that should have been demolished, not romanticized. The inn's weathered Victorian charm, which had felt like stepping into a storybook this morning, now looked merely old. The original wood floors that had seemed rich with history? She'd see water damage and poor maintenance. The mismatched china they'd used at breakfast? Evidence of a business that couldn't afford proper service sets.

"Hello, Marcus."

He turned, his body automatically assuming the posture she expected—shoulders back, chin up, the bearing of a Chen who understood his place in the world. "Mother. I wasn't expecting you."

"Clearly." Her gaze swept over him, cataloguing everything from his less-than-perfect tie to the way his hair fell naturally without that reeking gel. Behind her severe black suit and perfect chignon, the inn looked suddenly shabby, like a child's playhouse next to an actual home.

He bent to kiss her cheeks—the same ritual they'd performed for decades, affection reduced to obligation. Her perfume was unchanged from his childhood: Chanel No. 5, applied with surgical precision. Never too much, never too little. Like everything else about Dr. Helena Chen.

"You didn't return my calls," she said, making it sound like he'd committed a felony.

"I've been busy. It's Liam's wedding."

"Yes." She surveyed the reception with the same expression she used for substandard medical facilities. "Though I don't understand why Mei-Lin didn't insist on proper catering. These small-town affairs always try to do too much with too little."

The words hit exactly as intended. Suddenly he could see every homemade touch, every budget-conscious choice. Beatrice's lovingly prepared food looked amateur next to the Michelin-starred events his mother attended. The hothouse flower arrangements Katie had crafted seemed scraggly rather than charming.

"It's perfect," he said, but the words came out defensive rather than confident.

"If you say so." She swept him into the dining room, commandeering the table in the corner with the authority of someone used to the best seats simply appearing. "Sit. We need to discuss your interview."

"Mother—"

"Sit, Marcus."

Thirty-five years of training had him in the chair before he'd made the conscious decision to obey. Tom Carter was trying to decide if he should have a piece of the vanilla bride's cake or the chocolate groom's cake. How provincial, his mother would say. What would she said about the ice cream topping in the kitchen?

"Are you listening?" Helena's voice cut through his reverie.

"Sorry. What?"

"I said, your flight leaves Tuesday morning. I've already arranged everything with the hospital. Dr.

Matthews is eager to meet you, and the board is prepared to make an exceptional offer." She produced her phone, swiping to what looked like real estate listings. "I've found several suitable properties near UCSF. This one has an excellent view of the bay."

The house on the screen was everything she'd trained him to want—modern, pristine, with the kind of square footage that announced success. Looking at it, he felt nothing but a vague sense of suffocation.

"I haven't agreed to interview."

"Don't be ridiculous. Of course you have. I've already told them you're coming." She swiped to another listing. "This one's in Pacific Heights. The Morrison family lives three blocks away."

"The Morrison family?"

"Dr. Morrison from the surgical conference. His daughter Amy just finished her MBA at Harvard. Lovely girl. Very accomplished." Another swipe, this time to a LinkedIn profile. "She's expressed interest in meeting you."

Marcus stared at the professional headshot of a woman who looked like she'd been ordered from a catalog of Appropriate Life Partners. Harvard MBA, nonprofit board positions, the kind of smile that had been practiced in front of mirrors.

"No? Dr. McKhann's daughter just made partner at

Whitman Sterling. She's a little older, but…" Even mother's shrug was measured and graceful.

"You've been setting me up?" He tried to keep his voice down.

"I've been ensuring your future isn't derailed by…" Helena's gaze swept the room and found Kelsey with laser precision. "Distractions."

Heat flooded through him—anger and embarrassment and fierce protectiveness. "Her name is Kelsey."

"The photographer. From October." Helena made it sound like a temporary position that had been filled and was no longer needed. "Yes, Mei-Lin mentioned her. Pretty enough, I suppose, though that sort of bohemian lifestyle… Professional tourists, really, photographers. Never settling, always chasing the next pretty picture. Hardly conducive to a stable family life."

"You don't know anything about her."

"I know she doesn't have an advanced degree. Does she? I know she travels constantly for work. I know she's the type of woman who distracts brilliant men from their potential." Her tone was mild, conversational, as if she were discussing the weather rather than dissecting his choices. "You've worked too hard to throw it all away for someone you've known, what? A week?"

Eight days, his heart corrected.

Eight days that felt like a lifetime.

Eight days of her biting her lip when nervous, of her

laugh when she forgot to be guarded, of the way she looked at him like he was worth staying awake for.

Eight days that had shown him what he'd been missing.

But the words stuck in his throat because his mother was right about one thing—it wasn't long. Not in any way that made sense to someone like his mother.

"The interview is Wednesday," Helena continued, taking his silence for agreement. "We'll fly out Tuesday morning, get you settled at the hotel. The hospital tour is at two. Dinner with the board at seven. Thursday you can look at properties, and Friday..." She smiled, the expression not reaching her eyes. "The Morrisons are having a small dinner party. The perfect opportunity to meet Amy in a casual setting."

His life, scheduled and packaged and decided. No consultation, no consideration for what he might want. Just the assumption that he'd fall in line like he always had.

"What if I don't want to go?"

"What you want," Helena said with the patience of someone explaining basic concepts to a slow child, "is to waste your potential in small-town Michigan, playing handsy at your aunt's inn while your skills atrophy?"

The words landed like scalpels, precisely placed. Because wasn't that exactly what he'd been doing? Hiding from the career that was supposed to define him? Running from the expectations he'd been trained for since birth?

"I'm not playing anything. I'm—" What? Taking a break? Finding himself? Falling in love? All the explanations sounded childish in the face of her certainty.

"You're having a crisis," Helena said, almost gently. "It happens. That spinal case this week was difficult, I understand. But the answer isn't to throw away everything you've worked for. The answer is to push through, to achieve more, to prove that one failure doesn't define you."

One failure. Juliette Garcia reduced to a statistics point, a learning experience, a bump in his career trajectory. His hands clenched under the table.

Movement near the parlor entrance caught his eye. Kelsey was leaving, camera in hand, probably to photograph something. Or to escape. He started to rise, needing to explain, to warn her about his mother, to promise that none of this changed anything.

Helena's hand on his arm stopped him. "Where are you going?"

"I need to—"

"You need to focus on your future. Not chase after distractions."

"She's not a distraction."

"No?" Helena's smile was sharp. "Then what is she, Marcus? Your girlfriend? The woman you're building a future with? Or just someone you met at a wedding who'll be gone by February? Another professional tourist passing through?"

The question dangled between them like a blade. Because he didn't know.

They hadn't defined anything, hadn't made promises beyond tonight. Eight days of knowing each other, two months of missing each other, and what did that add up to? Not enough to throw away a career. Not enough to disappoint Helena Chen.

Not enough.

Except his whole body was screaming that it was everything, that Kelsey was everything, that the future his mother painted felt like death while eight uncertain days with a photographer felt like life.

"I need some air," he managed.

"Marcus—"

But he was already moving, ignoring his mother's disapproval burning into his back. He had to find Kelsey, had to explain. The reception swirled around him—laughter and music and happiness that felt suddenly foreign. Where was she?

He checked the hallway, empty. The kitchen, only staff. Finally spotted Katie coming from the lobby.

"Have you seen Kelsey?"

Katie's expression went carefully neutral in a way that made his stomach drop. "She needed a minute."

"Katie, please. I need to—"

"Your mom seems nice," Katie said with false brightness. "Very... planning-forward. I heard her mention the Morrison girl? Three times?"

Heat flooded his face. "That's not—I didn't ask for any of that."

"I know." Katie's voice gentled. "But Kelsey doesn't. All she sees is your mother planning your perfect life with your perfect future wife in your perfect San Francisco house."

"Where is she?"

Katie studied him for a long moment. "Porch. But Marcus? Maybe figure out what you're going to say first. Because 'sorry my mom's trying to arrange my marriage while we're dancing at someone else's wedding' isn't the strongest opener."

He found her near the dunes, the fading light making her glow like something from a painting. She had her camera up, photographing the view, but he could tell from the tension in her shoulders that she knew he was there. Only a mild wind, it wasn't too bad outside.

Except for why they were outside.

"I'm sorry," he said. "I didn't know she was coming."

"It's fine." She didn't lower the camera. "She's your mother. Of course she'd come to family events."

"Kelsey—"

"The Morrison girl sounds lovely." Her voice was carefully light. "Harvard MBA. Very impressive."

"I don't care about the Morrison girl."

"Your mother does." She finally lowered the camera but didn't turn to face him. "She's already got your whole life planned. The house, the career, the appropriate wife. Very tidy."

"That's not what I want."

"No?" She turned then, and the distance in her eyes made his chest tight. "What do you want, Marcus? Really? Because from where I'm standing, it looks like you want to rebel against mommy for a few weeks before falling back in line."

The words stung because they held enough truth to wound. "That's not fair."

"Isn't it?" She raised her camera again, up to her collarbone, using it as a shield between them. "We've known each other a total of eight days. Your mother's right about that. What kind of foundation is that for throwing away your whole future?"

"I'm not throwing away—"

"Aren't you? Chief of Emergency Medicine at UCSF is exactly the kind of position you've worked for your entire life. And you'd, what? Give that up for someone you barely know?"

"Stop saying that." The words came out harsher

than intended. "Stop acting like the time matters more than what we feel."

"What we feel?" She laughed, but it was brittle. "I feel confused. I feel like we're both caught up in wedding magic and starlight and really good kisses. I feel like in the harsh light of reality, none of this makes sense."

"You don't mean that."

"How do you know what I mean? You don't know me well enough—"

"I know you're scared." He stepped closer, watched her step back. "I know you use that camera like armor. I know you run when things get too real. I know you're looking for an excuse to leave before it hurts."

"And you're looking for an excuse to stay before you have to choose." Her voice cracked on the last word. "But you will have to choose, Marcus. Tuesday morning, you'll get on that plane or you won't. You'll interview for the job you've trained for your whole life or you won't. You'll meet the Morrison girl with her Harvard MBA and her appropriate pedigree or you won't."

"I would choose you." The words burst out of him, desperate and true. "I choose—"

"Eight days," she interrupted. "You choose eight days and some really spectacular kisses and the fantasy of something that might not even be real."

They stood there, three feet apart but feeling like

miles, both breathing hard. The lighthouse was dormant, offering no magical intervention. Just two people on a snow-strewn dune, trying to bridge the gap between what they felt and what made sense.

"Marcus?" His mother's voice from the doorway, perfectly timed as always. "There you are."

Helena stepped onto the porch with the confidence of someone who owned every space she entered. Her gaze dismissed Kelsey without a word, focusing on her son with laser intensity.

"We need to discuss your flight. The car will pick you up at seven Tuesday morning." She said it like it was already decided, already done. No question of whether he was going, just the logistics of compliance.

Marcus felt Kelsey withdrawing even though she hadn't moved. Saw her raising her camera again, documenting rather than participating. Already leaving even while standing still.

"I should get back to work," she said quietly. "Lots more to photograph."

"Kelsey—"

But she was already moving past him, careful not to touch. He took an instinctive step to follow, his whole body protesting the distance growing between them. His hands clenched into fists, chest tight like he couldn't breathe properly, every nerve ending screaming at him to go after her, to fix this, to not let her walk away thinking she didn't matter.

But he stayed where he was.

He watched her go, memorizing the set of her shoulders, the way she gripped her camera like a lifeline, the slight tremor in her hands that told him she was fighting tears. Eight days. Eight days of watching her bite her lip in concentration, of seeing her eyes light up when she captured the perfect shot, of learning that she organized her equipment when anxious and that she hummed off-key when she thought no one was listening.

"Honestly, Marcus," Helena said once they were alone. "A photographer? I thought I raised you to have higher standards."

The words ignited something in him. "You raised me to recognize quality when I see it. Kelsey has more integrity in her little finger than anyone at your hospital galas."

Helena's eyebrows rose slightly—the equivalent of shock from someone who'd perfected emotional control. "Careful, Marcus. You're being emotional."

"Maybe I want to be emotional. Maybe I'm tired of measuring everything by your standards of success."

"My standards?" Her voice went dangerously quiet. "You mean excellence? Achievement? Making a difference in the world?"

"I mean choosing career over connection. Success

over happiness. Being respected rather than being loved."

"And this photographer loves you?" Helena's smile was pitying. "After eight days? Oh, Marcus."

Eight days. But in those eight days, she'd made him laugh more than he had in months. Made him feel more like himself than he had in years. Made him believe in magic and possibility and futures that weren't planned in spreadsheets. Made him understand what his father had felt, why he'd fought for something beyond Helena's ambitious timeline.

"Did you ever wonder," he asked quietly, "if you chose wrong?"

"I chose excellence," she said without hesitation. "I chose to make a difference. I chose not to be distracted by temporary feelings that would have derailed everything I could become."

"And Dad? Was he just a temporary feeling?"

Something flickered across her face—there and gone too fast to read. "Your father understood the demands of excellence. Until he didn't."

"Until you pushed him away."

"Until he asked me to be less than I was." Her voice went sharp. "Is that what you want? To be less? To play house in small-town Michigan while your skills decay and your potential withers?"

Through the tall windows, he could see the reception continuing. Liam and Ella dancing again, lost in each other. His aunt laughing at something Agnes said. Kelsey in the corner, camera up, catching moments of joy while standing apart from them.

Everything was slipping away. He could feel it—the magic of last night dissolving under the weight of real world expectations. Eight days. It wasn't enough to build a life on. Wasn't enough to throw away everything he'd worked for.

Was it?

"Monday morning," Helena said, taking his silence for agreement. "Don't be late."

She left him on the porch, caught between two worlds that felt increasingly impossible to bridge. She didn't even go back inside.

Inside, where Kelsey was shooting candids of the dancing, her professional smile in place. When she glanced his way, the distance in her eyes was like a physical blow.

The lighthouse stood dark against the winter sky, no magic forthcoming. Just a defunct structure that used to guide ships home, now useful only as a reminder of what once was.

Marcus stood there, feeling the weight of choosing pressing down on him. Tuesday morning. The flight to his real life, or the chance at something that might not even survive February.

Eight days. His mother was right—it wasn't enough. It was everything.

He pulled out his phone, stared at Kelsey's name in his contacts. Started typing: *Please don't leave. Not yet. Not like this*

Deleted it. Typed: *I'm not getting on that plane*

Deleted it.

Inside, the photographer from October raised her camera toward the happy families, and even from here he could see her hands weren't steady.

Eight days. Not enough for certainty. But maybe enough for courage.

If he could find it before Monday.

Chapter Fourteen

The wedding reception had shifted into its evening rhythm—softer music, dimmed lights, the satisfied exhaustion of a celebration winding down. Kelsey moved through it like a ghost with a camera, documenting joy she couldn't feel. Her cheeks ached from her professional smile, and her hands had finally stopped shaking enough to hold the camera steady.

Don't think about the lighthouse. Don't think about Tuesday. Don't think about Marcus out there in the snow, looking inside like some little lost match boy.

She'd gotten good at not thinking in the half-hour since their dune confrontation. Good at focusing on f-stops and composition and the way candlelight caught on champagne flutes. Good at pretending her chest didn't feel hollowed out, like someone had scooped out everything vital and left her empty.

The inn, however, wasn't cooperating with her emotional avoidance.

Every door she tried to use stuck just long enough to make her struggle. The lights kept dimming when she tried to review photos, brightening aggressively when she tried to hide in shadows. Even her camera seemed rebellious—the usually reliable autofocus hunting and seeking, forcing her to manual mode.

"Having trouble?" Agnes appeared at her elbow with supernatural timing.

"Just the camera acting up." Kelsey fiddled with settings that hadn't need adjusting a second ago.

"Hmm." Agnes studied her with those sharp eyes that missed nothing. "Inn gets fussy when people are being stubborn."

As if to prove the point, the the sconce lights in the parlor flickered, sending shadows dancing across the walls and shouts out to Liam to "get to those fuses, husband-man!"

"I'm not being stubborn. I'm working," Kelsey said.

"If you say so."

By nine o'clock, Kelsey had documented every possible reception moment twice. The cake cutting (again, from new angles), the bouquet toss (caught by a delighted teenager), the garter ceremony (Katie's girlfriend blushing furiously), and approximately seventeen thousand candid moments of joy she couldn't feel.

Her feet hurt in her professional heels, her face ached from smiling, and she'd successfully avoided being within ten feet of Marcus for the past hour. A personal record, considering they were in the same room.

She was reviewing images on her camera's display, tucked safely behind a potted plant, when Beatrice materialized like a flour-dusted fairy godmother.

"Oh good, there you are! I need a favor, dear."

"Of course." Kelsey lowered her camera, grateful for any distraction.

"Would you mind photographing the wine selection in the cellar? For the inn's website. We're updating our romance package offerings, and potential guests love those behind-the-scenes touches."

It seemed odd to do it during a reception, but Kelsey wasn't about to argue with an excuse to escape. "Sure. Where's the cellar?"

"Through the kitchen, down the narrow stairs. Mind your head—those steps were built in 1902 when people were shorter." Beatrice beamed. "Take your time. Get creative shots. The lighting down there is very atmospheric."

Kelsey made her way through the kitchen, where the extra staff was already cleaning up. The cellar door stood open, revealing stone steps that descended into cool darkness. She hadn't noticed it there before. From below, she could smell aged wood and the faint mineral scent of old basements.

The stairs were indeed narrow, forcing her to go sideways in places. Original bare bulbs provided pools of yellow light between stretches of shadow. At the bottom, the cellar opened into a surprisingly high, large space with stone walls and wooden wine racks that looked as old as the inn itself.

"Atmospheric" was underselling it. The space felt like stepping back in time—cobwebs in corners, dust motes dancing in the thin light, bottles whose labels had faded to illegibility. Perfect temperature, if you were a bottle of wine. She raised her camera, already composing shots, when footsteps on the stairs made her freeze.

"—ten bottles should be enough," Agnes's voice drifted down. "Just grab the champagne cases from the back section."

Kelsey's pulse jumped. She knew who Agnes was sending before he appeared, sideways on the narrow stairs, looking as thrilled about this errand as she felt.

He looked exhausted, his earlier polish worn down to raw edges. His tie was loose, his hair mussed like he'd been running his hands through it, and his eyes—God, his eyes were full of so much pain it made her chest ache.

They stared at each other, neither speaking. The footsteps above retreated, and then—

Click.

The door shut. The lock turned.

"Oh, you've got to be kidding me," Marcus muttered, racing back up the stairs. He tried the handle. Nothing. "Hello? Agnes!"

No response.

"Locked," he said unnecessarily.

"I gathered that." Kelsey clenched her hands, released them. Think. "Cell service?"

They both checked. Nothing.

"Someone will miss us eventually," Marcus said, but he didn't sound convinced.

The cellar suddenly felt much smaller. She was acutely aware of him—the way he rolled his shoulders when tense, the way his hair was still mussed from their dance, the way he kept not quite looking at her.

"You wanted champagne?" she asked, voice artificially bright.

"Apparently. You?"

"Wine photos. For the website."

"Ah."

Silence stretched between them, broken only by the distant creaking of old pipes. Kelsey raised her camera, determined to actually work, but her hands weren't steady. Every shot came out blurred.

"Here," Marcus said quietly, appearing at her elbow. "You're too tense. Breathe."

"I know how to use my own camera."

"I know you do." His voice was gentle, patient. "But you're shaking."

She was.

"The wine's not going anywhere," he continued. "Just... breathe."

She lowered the camera, closed her eyes, tried to find center. But all she could smell was him—cologne and champagne and that indefinable Marcus scent that made her want to lean in and never leave.

"I hate this," she whispered.

"Being locked in?"

"No." She opened her eyes, found him closer than expected. "I hate that you think you don't matter."

His expression shifted, something raw flickering across his features.

"Kelsey—"

"And I hate that I want to matter." The admission felt ripped from her chest. "I hate that eight days feels like everything. I hate that your mother's right about me being a distraction. I hate that I can't just take the job and leave and not look back like I always do."

"What job?"

He hadn't heard. Of course he hadn't—she hadn't told him. It had all happened so fast.

"Maine Maritime Museum wants me. To be Director of Lighthouse Documentation."

"Wow." He looked stunned. Let go of her elbow. Tried to run his hand through his hair and hit a low-hanging pipe instead. "Wow."

"Richard—head of the board there—he called tonight. During the reception. I just found out."

"A real title," he said. "Respect. Salary?"

"Good salary. Housing, even." Saying it out loud really did make it sound good.

So why did she feel so bad?

He took her hand. His was so warm.

"Maine."

"San Francisco."

"I don't want you to leave." His voice was rough.

"But you're not asking me to stay either."

"How can I? How can I ask you to give up a career opportunity for someone you've known—"

"Eight days, I know." She laughed bitterly. "We keep coming back to that."

"Because it matters!"

"Does it?" She set her camera carefully on a wine crate, needing her hands free. "Does time matter more than this?" She gestured between them. "Than the way you look at me? Than how I feel when—"

He moved so fast she didn't see it coming. One moment they were three feet apart, the next he was crowding her against the wine rack, his hands framing her face.

"Don't," he said desperately. "Don't make this harder."

"How could it possibly be harder?"

They stared at each other, both breathing too fast. His thumb stroked her cheekbone, and she felt the touch everywhere.

"I love you," he said suddenly, the words falling between them like stones in still water. "I'm in love with you. Eight days, two months, I don't care. I love you, and it's killing me that you think you're just a distraction."

Her breath caught. "Marcus—"

"No, let me finish. I've been trying to be logical, trying to make this make sense, but love doesn't make sense. My parents were together fifteen years before my mom chose her career over marriage. Sarah knew Harold two weeks. Time doesn't guarantee anything."

"We're not your parents. Or Sarah and Harold."

"Then what are we doing?" His forehead dropped to rest against hers. "Tell me what we're doing, because I can't figure it out."

"Maine Maritime wants an answer by Tuesday."

His hands tightened infinitesimally on her face. "Same as my interview."

"I love you too," she breathed, and felt him shudder. "I love you. So much it terrifies me."

"Kelsey—"

Pounding on the door shattered the moment.

"Marcus?" Tom's voice, muffled through the door.

They sprang apart like guilty teenagers. Marcus cleared his throat. "We're locked in."

"Are you now?" Tom sounded suspiciously unsurprised. "Let me just find the right key..."

The lock clicked, the door opened, and Tom appeared with an expression of studied innocence. "Found it. First try. Lucky."

"Miraculous," Marcus said dryly.

Kelsey grabbed her camera, pushing past both men. "I should get back."

"Kelsey—" Marcus started.

"The reception," she said without turning. "I'm working."

"You're off the clock," Tom called after her. "Everybody's packing it up."

Kelsey fled up the stairs, through the kitchen, up more stairs, down the hall, into her room. Into the bathroom where she could lean against the sink and splash cold water on her burning face. In the mirror, she looked wrecked—lips swollen from biting them, eyes too bright, that telltale flush that screamed "almost kissed in a wine cellar."

Her phone buzzed. Marcus: *Can we talk? Really talk?*

She stared at the message, fingers hovering over the keyboard. Typed: *After. When everyone's gone.*

Deleted it.

Typed: *What's left to say?*

Deleted that too.

Finally sent: *Library? Midnight*

His response was immediate: *I'll be there.*

Chapter Fifteen

The library was dark, the waning moon just a pale sliver, when Kelsey arrived. One lamp was lit near the two wingback chairs by the fireplace, but no one was there.

She'd changed into jeans and a soft sweater, needing comfort more than professionalism. Still, she felt naked. She'd left her cameras in her room.

She didn't want the shield of her lens between her and whatever came next.

Marcus was already there, standing by the windows with his back to her. He'd changed too—khakis and a pullover that made him look younger, less like Dr. Chen and more like the Marcus who'd shared hot chocolate on a snowy beach.

"Hi," she said softly.

He turned, and the hope in his eyes nearly undid her. "You came."

"I said I would."

"I know. I just..." He ran a hand through his already messed hair. "I wasn't sure."

They stood there, the width of the library between them, both afraid to close the distance. Through the windows, the lighthouse beam swept steadily across the water, painting silver paths in the darkness.

"I've been thinking," they both said at once, then stopped.

"You first," Kelsey said.

Marcus moved toward the chairs, pulling a legal pad from the seam of one. Even in the The first page was covered in his neat handwriting.

"I couldn't sleep," he said. "So I started researching. Making lists. Trying to find a way through this that isn't either/or."

She moved closer, drawn despite herself. "What kind of lists?"

"Everything. Hospitals in Boston—it's four hours from northern Maine. Portland has three major medical centers, and it's only two and a half hours to Boston." He dropped into the chair, to get more light on the paper. "I looked at flights, drive times, even train schedules." He looked up at her, vulnerability naked on his face. "I know it sounds desperate—"

"It sounds like fighting," she said softly. She pulled the other chair closer to his, and sank into it. "You're actually fighting for us."

"Of course I am." He set the pad aside, turning to face her fully. "Kelsey, I meant what I said in the cellar. I love you. And I know eight days isn't long enough to make life decisions, but it's long enough to know I want the chance to try."

She felt tears prick her eyes. "I love you too. But—"

"No." He took her hands, gentle but firm. "No buts. Not yet. Just... let me show you something."

He pulled out his phone, showing her an email. "I wrote to the hiring committee at UCSF. Told them I need to postpone the interview."

Her breath caught. "Marcus, your mother—"

"Will be furious. But this is my life, not hers." He squeezed her hands. "I also reached out to a colleague at Mass General. They have a trauma fellowship starting in July. Boston, Kelsey. Close enough to Maine for weekends. Close enough to figure out what comes next."

"You'd give up San Francisco? The deputy chief position?"

"I'd give up anything that meant choosing career over you." His thumb stroked over her knuckles. "My mother chose ambition over love. I watched what it did to my father, to our family. I won't make the same mistake."

Kelsey felt something crack open in her chest—the walls she'd built around her heart, the certainty that leaving was safer than staying.

"I don't know how to do this," she admitted. "I've spent my whole life leaving before it could hurt."

He brought her hands to his lips, kissing each palm. "Stay. Fight with me. We'll figure out the geography, the jobs, all of it. We'll figure it out together."

The lighthouse beam swept across them, illuminating the hope and fear on both their faces. The inn was hushed; only the radiator gurgled its winter melody.

"Richard wants an answer by Tuesday," she said.

"So does my mother. Guess we both have difficult phone calls to make."

"What if..." She took a breath, gathering courage. "What if I took the job but negotiated? Asked for flexibility, for remote work options? Maine to Boston is manageable, especially if you're there."

His face lit up. "You'd consider Boston?"

"I'd consider Mars if it meant we could try this." She loved his laugh. "But Boston seems more practical."

"Extremely practical. Very us." He pulled her closer, their foreheads touching. "Look at us being adult about this. Making plans. Finding compromise."

"It's disgusting," she agreed, but she was smiling. "What happened to running away at the first sign of feelings?"

"You fell in love with someone just as scared as you." He kissed her softly, sweetly. "Someone who thinks you're worth being brave for."

When they pulled apart, she asked, "What do we do now?"

"Now?" He stood, pulling her up with him. "Now we get some sleep." He rubbed his forehead. Then tomorrow, we make some phone calls. Face some dragons. Start building something real."

"Together?"

"Together."

They walked the long second-floor hall from the library to the great stairs hand-in-hand. At Kelsey's door, Marcus kissed her again, lingering and sweet.

"No running away in the night?"

"No running," she promised.

"Good." He backed toward his room, smiling. "Because I meant what I said. I'd chase you to Mars."

"Boston will be far enough," she said. "Goodnight."

"Goodnight, Kelsey. See you at breakfast. We can practice our phone calls on each other."

She slipped into her room, but instead of packing, she unpacked. Hung clothes in the wardrobe. Set her cameras on the dresser. Small acts of staying, of choosing to believe in tomorrow.

Through her window, the lighthouse had gone dark, its job complete. But Kelsey didn't need its light anymore. She'd found her own way home—not to a place, but to a person who made staying worth the risk.

Eight days. A lifetime.

When you know, you know.

Love was worth fighting for, even when the path wasn't clear. Marcus had shown her that tonight—not with grand gestures or desperate pleas, but with train schedules and research and the quiet determination of someone who refused to let either/or be the only option.

Tomorrow would bring difficult conversations and complicated logistics. But tonight, she fell asleep smiling, knowing that somewhere across the hall, the man she loved was probably making more lists in his dreams. Finding more solutions Fighting for their future with the same meticulous care he brought to everything that mattered.

They'd figure it out. Together.

Chapter Sixteen

The big kitchen table at nine in the morning held hope and exhaustion and too many empty coffee cups. Marcus had pulled out his laptop, Kelsey had her phone, and between them lay a legal pad filled with increasingly wild ideas—some crossed out, some circled, some decorated with question marks.

"Commuter marriage?" Kelsey read from the list. "Marcus, Portland to San Francisco is not commutable."

"I know. I was getting desperate around 3 AM." He rubbed his eyes. She smelled so good. "What about the one where we both become lighthouse keepers?"

"Romantic but impractical."

"Story of us."

They reached for each other's hands under the table,

still amazed they were here, doing this, choosing the difficult path instead of the easy goodbye.

"Oh thank goodness!."

They looked up to find Ella in the doorway, four hours later than usual and still in her honeymoon glow. She took one look at them—shoulders touching, exhausted but together—and actually fist-pumped.

"Katie owes me fifty bucks." As if on stage, Katie swept in, looking well-rested and decidedly chipper."

"Seriously?" she said. "This wedding is getting expensive."

Ella came closer, assessing the situation with the efficiency of someone who'd recently planned a wedding in less than two months. "Okay, what do you need? A printer? Extra strength tea? A miracle? I have access to all three."

"A plan," Kelsey admitted. "We're trying to figure out how to make this work, but—"

"Library," Ella said decisively. "Better WiFi, more space, and I can lock the door if your mother shows up again." This to Marcus, who winced. "Also, you both need food. Real food, not just coffee and feelings."

Thirty minutes later, the library had been transformed into what Katie dubbed "Love's War Room." Laptops at one end of the large antique table, maps of the eastern seaboard over the other. Phones charging in every outlet. The inn had contributed by ensuring perfect coffee appeared whenever cups emptied and keeping the fire at exactly the right temperature.

"Boston," Liam said, pointing to the map. He also had that weird glow. Shouldn't these two be still in bed or wherever? But Marcus was glad he was here. That they all were.

Strength in numbers.

"It's the logical compromise," Ella said. Two and a half hours to Portland, major medical centers for Marcus, thriving arts scene for photography."

"When did you two get so romantic?" Katie teased, but she was already pulling up apartment listings on her tablet.

Marcus was deep in research on Boston teaching hospitals, his concentration face making Kelsey want to kiss him despite their audience. She forced herself to focus on her own laptop, emailing photography contacts about the Boston scene.

"Mass General has openings," Marcus announced. "Emergency department, looking for someone to start in July. That would give me time to finish residency, take boards—"

"July?" Kelsey's heart sank. "That's seven months away."

"Better than never," Ella said gently.

The library phone rang—an ancient rotary that Ella hadn't been sure even worked. Katie answered with suspicious cheer. "Love's War Room, how may we direct your call?"

She listened, her expression shifting. "It's for you," she said to Marcus. "Your mom. She sounds... displeased."

Marcus had ignored six calls already. On the seventh, with everyone watching, he finally answered his cell. "Hello, Mother."

"Your flight is in forty-eight hours." Helena's voice carried clearly through the speaker. "I haven't received confirmation that you've checked in."

"That's because I haven't. I'm exploring all options."

"Options?" The temperature in her voice could have frosted windows. "The only option is getting on that plane. Dr. Matthews—"

"Can find another candidate."

Silence. Then, deadly quiet: "This is about that photographer."

Everyone in the room bristled. Kelsey reached for Marcus's hand, but Ella beat them all to it, plucking the phone from Marcus's grip with newlywed confidence.

"Hi, Mrs. Dr. Chen? This is Ella Thompson Carter —we met yesterday at my wedding? I just wanted to say how much we appreciate Marcus here at the inn. Did you know he increased our maintenance efficiency by thirty percent? And our guest satisfaction scores are up fifteen percent since October. He's quite valuable to our operations."

"Who is this?" Helena's voice was sharp with confusion.

"Oh, I'm sorry, I should clarify. I own the Starlight Arbor Inn. We're actually considering expansion—Marcus has been invaluable in planning. Such a good eye for structural integrity. And of course, his medical knowledge has been wonderful for our elderly guests. Why, just last week he helped Mrs. Patterson with her heart medication timing."

"I... see." Helena sounded completely wrong-footed.

"We'd hate to lose him, of course. But we understand San Francisco's appeal. Though really, with telemedicine these days, location is so flexible, isn't it? Marcus could practice anywhere. Even Boston—lovely medical community there. Have you been? Wonderful lobster."

Katie was biting her fist to keep from laughing. Liam looked deeply appreciative of his wife's talent for aggressive kindness.

"Please put my son back on," Helena said finally.

"Of course! So lovely chatting with you. We must have tea sometime." Ella handed the phone back to Marcus with a beatific smile.

"Mother—"

"We'll discuss this when you get home."

"I *am* home."

The words hung there, simple and true.

Helena hung up without another word.

"That," Katie said to Ella, "was magnificent."

"I learned from the best." Ella glanced at the portrait of Sarah watching over them all. "Kill them with kindness and inn statistics."

Marcus's phone immediately buzzed with texts, but he turned it face down. "She'll call back. Probably with PowerPoints."

"Then we'd better have better ones," Kelsey said, surprised at the determination in her voice. The fierceness. "What else do we need to figure out?"

Richard, and the Maine Maritime Museum. She couldn't put it off

"Okay," she said, pulling out her phone. "Richard first. If I'm going to completely upend his plans, I should do it before he's had too much coffee."

Marcus squeezed her hand. "Want me to go?"

"No. Stay." She took a breath. "We're doing this together, right?"

She dialed, putting it on speaker. The gathered family tried to look like they weren't eagerly eavesdropping.

"Kelsey! Perfect timing. I was just about to call you about—"

"Richard, I accept the position," she said quickly. "But I need to talk to you about Boston."

Silence. Then: "Boston? Kelsey, the position is in Portland. The whole point is documenting the Maine lighthouses."

"I know. And I want the job. But..." She glanced at Marcus, who nodded encouragingly. "My circumstances have changed. I need to be based in Boston."

"Changed how?" Richard's voice had gone careful. "Kelsey, this position was designed specifically for you. The board—"

"The person I'm in love with will be in Boston." The words came out in a rush. "Starting in July. And I know it's only been—time doesn't matter. What matters is I'll do better work if I'm happy. And I'll be happy if I can be near him."

Katie made a silent 'aww' face. Ella nodded approvingly. Even Liam had stopped pretending to study his laptop.

"The lighthouse preservation project needs someone who understands these structures," Kelsey continued, her professional voice strengthening. "I can do that from Boston. Site visits, documentation trips—Maine's what, two hours? I'll spend whatever time on-site you need. But my home base needs to be Boston."

"Kelsey..." Richard sighed. "You're asking me to

completely restructure a position we've been developing for months."

"I know." Her free hand clenched. "And if you can't, I understand. We could ease into it, even. Me in Maine for the January 15th project, and then in Boston by summer. But I have to ask. Because this—he—it's worth asking for."

Marcus lifted their joined hands and kissed her knuckles. Across the table, Ella made a soft sound.

"You're really going to turn down your dream job for some man you just met?" Richard sounded more curious than condemning.

"No," Kelsey said firmly. "I'm asking you to let me have both. The dream job and the dream guy. And he's not just some man. He's—" She looked at Marcus. "He's the person who makes me want to stay somewhere for the first time in my life."

Another long pause. Beatrice had stopped pretending to fuss with the coffee pot. Everyone was holding their breath.

"MIT," Richard said finally.

"What?"

"MIT has been after us to partner on urban lighthouse preservation. Mapping how lighthouse technology influenced harbor development. Boston Harbor Light, Graves Light, Minot's Ledge..." They could hear papers shuffling. "If you were in Boston, you could lead that partnership."

"Richard—"

"It's different than what we planned. The board won't love it. But if you can sell them on the MIT connection, the academic prestige…" Another pause. "You'd still need to cover the Maine sites. Monthly trips minimum."

"Yes. Absolutely. Whatever you need."

"And the salary might be less initially. Boston's expensive, and restructuring the position—"

"I don't care about the money," Kelsey said, then caught herself. "I mean, I care, but not more than—"

"I know what you mean." Richard's voice had warmed. "Email me a formal proposal. Include the MIT angle. I'll take it to the board Tuesday."

"Richard, I—thank you. Thank you so much."

"Don't thank me yet. The board still has to approve it. But Kelsey? I've seen your work. You're happiest when you're emotionally connected to your subjects. If this person makes you happy…" He chuckled. "Just make sure he's worth reorganizing an entire museum project for."

"He is," she said, looking directly at Marcus. "He absolutely is."

After she hung up, the room exploded. Katie actually cheered. Beatrice burst into tears. Ella nodded like she'd personally orchestrated the whole thing.

"Wait," Kelsey said. "That was just the first step. Richard still has to convince the board—"

"He'll convince them," Ella said confidently. "The inn's on your side. That counts for something."

As if in agreement, the coffee pot burbled happily

Marcus smiled. "See? The inn has spoken. Now, my turn. Though mine's not as exciting. Just an email since I've never actually talked to anyone there except through my mother."

"What are you going to say?" Ella asked.

Marcus's fingers tapped fast, Morse-coding the keys. "Dear Dr. Matthews, Thank you for considering me for the position of Deputy Chief of Emergency Medicine. After careful consideration of my personal and professional goals, I must respectfully withdraw from consideration. I appreciate your time and wish you success in finding the right candidate. Sincerely, Dr. Marcus Chen."

"That's it?" Katie peered over his shoulder. "No explanation?"

"They don't need one. This was always more my mother's dream than mine." He hit send before he could second-guess himself. "Done."

Kelsey squeezed his hand. "How does it feel?"

"Like I can breathe for the first time in years." He

turned to face the room. "We should probably prepare for—"

His phone rang. Helena.

"That was fast," Liam observed. "She probably has alerts set up on my email," Marcus said, only half-joking. He declined the call. "She can wait. We're planning our future here."

They continued working through the morning, refining their plan with concrete next steps and fresh cinnamon rolls. Boston as base was no longer just a hope—Richard was taking it to the board, and Marcus had officially declined San Francisco. He'd apply for positions around Boston as he finished his Chicago residency.

The plan looked less like a wild hope and more like an actual future. Six months of long distance, then together.

Not perfect. But possible.

Around noon, when they were debating the merits of various Boston neighborhoods (Katie voting for wherever had the best coffee shops), Mei-Lin Frankl appeared in the doorway.

"If you're going to fight Helena," she said without preamble, "you need better weapons than Google and optimism."

She moved into the room with elegant authority,

scanning the research scattered across the table. "Marcus, walk with me."

He glanced at Kelsey, who nodded. Sometimes battles had to be fought alone before they could be won together.

Mei-Lin led him to her private sitting room, the one tourists never saw. It smelled of jasmine tea and old incense, every surface holding careful treasures from a life lived between two cultures.

"Your mother called," she said, settling into her chair. "Three times."

"I'm sorry—"

"Don't apologize for choosing happiness." She reached into an antique desk, withdrawing an envelope. "Your mother never told you why I left Beijing."

Marcus blinked at the shift. "You came for nursing school."

"That's what we told people." Mei-Lin smiled. "The truth was simpler and more complicated. I fell in love with an American soldier. Our father—your grandfather—was a professor at Beijing University. Tenured. Respected. Revolutionary in his own way."

She handed him a photograph—a young Chinese man in professor's robes standing next to a woman in a nurse's uniform. They were smiling like they knew all the world's secrets.

"He gave it up. Tenure, respect, his entire life—to

follow my mother to America. Started over as a high school math teacher in Michigan. Never made full professor again. Never published another paper."

"Did he regret it?"

"Every day," Mei-Lin said, and Marcus's heart sank. "He regretted the papers he didn't write, the students he didn't teach, the accolades he didn't receive. But Marcus —" She leaned forward. "He said the regret was like background music. Barely audible under the symphony of the life he chose."

She pressed another envelope into his hands. "Your mother never forgave him for choosing love over prestige. Don't let her make you the same."

Marcus recognized the handwriting. His father's careful script, addressed to him.

"He asked me to give this to you when you were ready," Mei-Lin said softly. "I think perhaps you are."

Marcus's hands shook as he opened the letter.

My dear son,

If Mei-Lin has given you this, then you're facing the choice I faced twenty years ago. I know your mother has told you I was weak, that I chose the easy path. But Marcus, there's nothing easy about choosing happiness in a world that measures worth in achievements.

I spent twenty years trying to make her see that music was as valuable as medicine, that teaching children to create beauty mattered as much as saving lives. But she could never see past the lesser salary, the smaller reputation, the lack of publications.

I didn't leave her, son. I left the fight. I was tired of defending my joy.

Your mother saves lives. It's noble work. But make sure, my boy, that you live yours.

Whatever choice you're facing, ask yourself: Will I regret this more than I'll regret the alternative? And remember—careers can be rebuilt. Love, real love, is rarer than any job title.

Be braver than I was. Choose sooner. Fight harder.

All my love, Dad

Marcus read it twice, tears blurring the words. All those years of careful distance between his parents, and here was the truth—not that his father wasn't enough, but that his mother couldn't see he was more than enough.

He found Kelsey on the porch, taking a break from the war room by standing in the sunny cold. She was photographing the lighthouse in afternoon sun, but lowered her camera when she saw his face.

"What happened?"

He showed her the letter. He watched her read it, watched her eyes fill. When she finished, she swung her camera around to the back and pulled him into her arms.

"Your dad sounds wonderful." Her breath puffed soft against his cheek.

"He is. I should call him. Tell him—" Marcus paused. "Tell him I understand now."

They stood together, looking out at the lighthouse that had started everything. It stood patient in the winter sun, waiting for darkness to return to its work.

"I need to text Richard," Kelsey said suddenly. "Thank him again. Make sure he has everything he needs for the board." She laughed, slightly hysterical. "Are we really doing this?"

"We're really doing this." He pulled her close. "Is that okay?"

"It's terrifying."

"And?"

"And perfect."

They were still embracing when the porch door burst open. Katie skidded to a stop. "Code Helena! She's here! At the front desk! Agnes is stalling but—"

Marcus's blood chilled.

"Let's go," Kelsey said, taking his hand. "Together, remember?"

They found Helena in the parlor, seated on a velvet sofa amidst the crooked ribbons and tilted flower arrangements of yesterday's wedding, looking like corporate judgment in her black suit. Agnes hovered nearby, clearly ready to intervene if needed. The rest of their war room team had mysteriously appeared—Ella perched on the arm of the facing sofa arm, Liam standing protective behind her, Katie lurking by the door.

Mei-Lin, moving fast, came in from the dining room. She stopped short, and leaned against the doorway, trying to catch her breath. In a wool coat and mittens, she must have just come in from outside.

Helena did not acknowledge her. "Marcus." Her voice could have cut glass. "We need to talk. Alone."

"No." The word came out steadier than he felt. "Whatever you need to say can be said in front of Kelsey."

Helena's gaze flicked dismissively over Kelsey, then back to him. "Fine. I've spoken to Dr. Matthews. He's willing to hold the position until Thursday, given your excellent record. This gives you time to come to your senses."

"My senses are fine."

"Are they?" She stood gracefully and stepped closer to him. Marcus fought the instinct to stand straighter, to become the dutiful son she expected. "You're throwing away everything we've worked for. Everything I've sacrificed to give you."

"Everything you've sacrificed," Marcus repeated. "What about what I'm sacrificing?"

"What could you possibly be sacrificing by accepting one of the most prestigious positions in the country?"

"Happiness," he said simply. "Love. A life that feels like mine instead of yours."

Helena's perfect composure cracked. "Love? You've known this woman a week."

"Eight days," Kelsey said quietly. "And two months of missing each other. And hopefully a lifetime of choosing each other."

Helena turned the full force of her attention on Kelsey. "And when this falls apart? When he resents you for the career he gave up? When you're struggling with bills because he's at some community hospital instead of leading departments?"

"Then we'll handle it together," Kelsey said, stepping forward. "Like adults who chose each other with eyes wide open."

"You're selfish."

"Yes," Kelsey agreed, surprising everyone, including herself. "I'm selfish. But so are you. You want Marcus to live your dream, not his. You want him to achieve what you think matters. That's not love, Dr. Chen. That's control."

Helena went very still. "How dare you—"

"She's right." Marcus's voice was quiet but firm. "You've been living through me since Dad left. Every achievement, every accolade—it was for you, not me."

"Everything I've done has been for you!"

"No. It's been for the version of me you wanted.

The son who would prove your choices were right. That choosing career over family was noble instead of just... lonely."

Helena flinched as if struck. "I am not lonely."

Mei-Lin sank onto the other sofa, sighing. Helena did not even glance at her sister.

"When's the last time someone hugged you?" Marcus asked gently. "When's the last time you had dinner with someone who wasn't a colleague? When's the last time you were happy?"

"Happiness is not the measure of a life well-lived."

"Then what is?" He moved closer to his tiny powerhouse of a mother, seeing her clearly for perhaps the first time. "Publications? Awards? An empty house full of achievements?"

"If you do this," Helena said, her voice shaking slightly, "don't expect me to pick up the pieces when it falls apart. Don't come running home when—"

"This is home," Marcus interrupted. "Here. With these people. With Kelsey. You're welcome to be part of it, but I'm not leaving it for anything. Not even for you."

Helena's face went through several expressions— fury, hurt, something that might have been grief. "Then I suppose we have nothing more to say to each other."

"Mom—"

"No." She held up a hand. "You've made your

choice. You'd rather play small-town doctor with your photographer than become what you could be. Fine. But don't call me when you realize what you've thrown away. Don't expect me at your wedding—if it even gets that far. Don't..."

Her voice broke slightly. She gathered herself, that perfect composure sliding back into place like armor.

"Don't expect me to watch you waste everything I've sacrificed to give you."

She left without another word, her heels clicking on the inn's old floors with finality. The sound faded, leaving behind a silence that felt heavier than before.

"She'll come around," Mei-Lin said softly. "When she sees your happiness—"

"No," Marcus said, staring at the door. "She won't. That's the price."

Mei-Lin rose equally gracefully, despite the bulky wool coat. "Perhaps. Perhaps not. Six decades is a long time to be sisters. Excuse me."

She moved toward the door with quiet purpose. From the lobby, Mei-Lin's voice carried back, gentle but insistent: "Helena. A moment."

A pause.

"Tea," Mei-Lin said simply. "You've driven all this way. At least have tea with your sister before you go."

"I have nothing to say to you."

"Then I'll talk. About Father. About choices. About

the price of being right versus being happy." Mei-Lin sighed. "One cup, Helena. You owe me that much."

"Not here."

"Down in town, then."

"Fine."

They heard the outer door open and click shut.

"Well," Katie said into the silence. "That's something."

"Your aunt is formidable," Kelsey said.

"She is." Marcus said. "But changing Helena's mind... that would take an actual miracle." He dragged a hand through his hair, and then cupped the back of his neck.

"Come on," Kelsey said, tugging his other hand. "Let's go back to our planning. We have a future to build, with or without your mother's approval."

He looked at her—this woman who'd stood up to Helena Chen without flinching, who'd rearranged her entire career for them, who was choosing him despite the mess of his family—and felt his chest ease.

"You're right. We do." He kissed her quickly. "Thank you. For fighting beside me."

"Always," she said. "That's what partners do."

That evening, the dining room was transformed for an impromptu celebration. Not as grand as the wedding, but somehow just as meaningful. Their small circle of family, chosen and otherwise. Beatrice had outdone herself with comfort food, Agnes had brought out wines from the private collection, and Mei-Lin was slightly drunk.

"To brave choices," Ella toasted, raising her glass.

"To foolish love," Katie added.

"To fighting for happiness," Mei-Lin contributed.

"To Tuesday," Marcus said, looking at Kelsey. "And whatever comes after."

They drank, they laughed, they planned. Boston was becoming real—neighborhoods discussed, logistics debated, even furniture shopping planned (Katie's favorite part). The impossibility of the morning was becoming possibility with each passing hour.

After dinner, Marcus and Kelsey escaped to the beach. Their beach now, site of so many conversations and kisses and almosts. The lighthouse was already on, painting the snow silver, but tonight it felt like celebration rather than warning.

"Six months," Kelsey said, leaning into his warmth. "Richard texted. If Boston approves, I start in January, but you can't move until next July. Six months of long distance."

"We did two months of complete silence and survived," he pointed out.

"That was different. We weren't together then. Now…" She turned to face him. "Now I know what I'm missing. What if the distance is too hard? What if we can't—"

"Hey." He cupped her face. "We'll have visits. Weekends. Terrible video calls where the connection drops every five minutes."

"Your mother might be right—"

"My mother," he said, firm, "doesn't get to decide what's possible for us."

"But six months, Marcus. And I'll be making less money because of the relocation costs. And you'll be finishing residency on no sleep. And—"

He kissed her to stop the spiral. When he pulled back, her eyes were wet.

"You're going to get icicles if you keep crying."

"I'm scared," she admitted.

"Me too. But I'm more scared of not trying."

"You. Me. Building something worth keeping." He kissed her, soft and sure. "I love you. That's the point."

"I love you too." The words still felt new to her, precious. "Enough to try Boston. Enough to try long distance. Enough to try scary and uncertain and—"

He kissed her again, deeper this time, and she forgot what she was saying. Forgot everything except the warmth of him, the rightness of choosing this, choosing them.

"Come on," he said finally, pulling back. "It's freezing, and we have even more calls to make tomorrow."

They walked back hand in hand, the lighthouse beam following their progress like a benediction. Tomorrow would bring difficult conversations—Kelsey officially accepting the position with modifications, Marcus withdrawing from San Francisco, both of them figuring out the intricate dance of two careers and one love.

But tonight, they had each other and a plan and a family that had fought alongside them all day.

At the inn's entrance, Marcus paused. "Your room or mine?"

The question hung between them, new territory in their careful courtship.

"Yours," she decided. "Mine's full of half-packed equipment and anxiety."

His room welcomed them with warmth and that particular Marcus scent of soap and cologne and possibility. Kelsey set her camera on the dresser—she didn't need to document this. Some moments were for living, not capturing.

They came together slowly, carefully, each touch a question and answer. But between them lay the weight of what they'd sacrificed—her original position, his mother's approval, the easier paths they'd both rejected.

"Do you think we're making a mistake?" she whispered in the darkness.

"Maybe," he admitted, and felt her tense. "But I'd rather make this mistake with you than make the safe choice alone."

She was quiet for so long he thought she'd fallen asleep. Then: "I've never turned down a job for someone before. I've never chosen to stay. What if I'm bad at it?"

"Then we'll be bad at it together."

"Your mom—"

"Made her choice. Just like we made ours." But his voice caught because the price was higher than he'd admitted downstairs. No mother at his wedding. No proud phone calls about achievements. No family except the one he was building here.

Kelsey seemed to understand. She pulled him closer, and they held each other in the darkness—two people who'd chosen love over logic, each other over everything else, knowing the price and paying it anyway.

"No regrets?" she asked.

"Ask me in a year," he said honestly. "When we've survived long distance and reduced salaries and all the things that could go wrong."

"And if we don't survive?"

"Then at least we tried. At least we were brave."

The lighthouse beam made another pass, and in its light, he saw tears on her cheeks that matched his own. This wasn't the triumphant movie moment. This was real life—messy and uncertain and full of prices to be paid.

"I love you," she said, fierce and determined. "That has to be enough."

"It is enough," he promised, hoping they were both right.

Whatever happened tomorrow, they'd face it together.

Eight days. Two months. Six months of distance. A lifetime of choosing each other over safer paths.

When you know, you know.

Love was worth fighting for, even when the fight cost everything else.

One imperfect, glorious day at a time.

Chapter Seventeen

Three months later

The kitchen at the Starlight Arbor Inn was in full rebellion. Where normally it hummed with the comfortable chaos of meal preparation, today it practically vibrated with conspiracy.

Kelsey stood at the scarred wooden table, her fingers sticky with frosting, trying to pipe "Happy Birthday" on what had to be Beatrice's fourth attempt at the perfect cake. Through the tall windows, March light filtered weak and watery, catching the steam that rose from multiple projects and fogged the old glass until the outside world became an impressionist painting.

"Don't say the B-word!" Beatrice shrieked, dropping

her spatula with a clatter that made everyone jump. Flour puffed up from where it hit the table, adding another layer to her already-dusted apron. "She has ears like a cat, that one."

"She's in town with Katie," Agnes said, not looking up from her military-precise arrangement of salad ingredients for the feast. "Has been for two hours. The library, the antique shop, and if Katie's smart, that new tea place that just opened." She consulted a list that looked like battle plans, complete with timing annotations. "We have until four."

The kitchen smelled like heaven had a nervous breakdown. Vanilla extract and cinnamon tangled with the sizzle of fried dough. Beatrice's three completed cakes—simple white, lemon, and what looked like red velvet—cooled on the counter, while something savory bubbled on the massive vintage stove. Its familiar temperamental humming had reached the pitch that meant someone needed to jiggle the back left burner before it went out entirely.

"Kelsey, dear, that's perfect," Cordelia said, looking up from her napkin origami. She'd transformed the cream-colored linens into a small army of swans, each one more elaborate than the last. "What about a little flower garland?"

"You do know," Kelsey said, contemplating piping a

scrollwork border without the correct frosting tip, "that we all of us won't be able to manage to eat one of these cakes, right?"

"Amateur," Agnes said, marking something off her list with surgical precision. "Watch and learn."

The copper pots hanging from the darkened oak beams stretched across the ceiling caught the afternoon light, turning it amber and warm despite the March winds pressing at the windows. Herbs dangled from one —rosemary and thyme and sage—their scents adding an earthy undertone to the sugar-sweet air.

This kitchen had become as familiar to Kelsey as her own cameras over the past months. She knew which floorboard creaked (second from the pantry), which chair wobbled (second from left), and exactly how Agnes liked her coffee (strong enough to strip paint, one sugar, no nonsense).

A car door slammed outside. Kelsey's hands stilled on the piping bag, her body recognizing the sound before her mind caught up. The particular way Marcus closed his Accord's door—firm but not aggressive, followed by the trunk opening for his overnight bag. Her pulse kicked up, skin warming with anticipation. Three weeks since she'd seen him in person. Three weeks of video calls and texts and falling asleep to his voice through phone speakers.

"He's here," Beatrice announced unnecessarily, peering through the foggy window. "Oh, he looks tired. That drive from Chicago in this weather—Agnes, is there soup hot? That boy needs soup."

"That boy needs to help with decorations," Agnes said, but she was already moving toward the stove, ladling something that smelled like comfort into a bowl.

The kitchen door opened, bringing a rush of cold air that smelled like snow and pine and Marcus. He stood in the doorway for a moment, overnight bag in one hand, taking in the controlled chaos. His navy coat was dusted with the light snow that had been falling all day, his glasses slightly fogged from the temperature change. The drive had left shadows under his eyes, but they lit up when they found her across the room.

"Hi," he said, and that one word carried three weeks of missing each other.

"Hi yourself." She set down the piping bag, wiping her hands on the apron Beatrice had insisted she wear. "Good drive?"

"Better now." He dropped his bag by the door and crossed to her in three strides, pulling her into a hug that felt like coming home.

He smelled like winter air and that unique combination of his cologne and car interior and something uniquely Marcus. She pressed her face into his snow-damp shoulder, breathing him in, feeling the tension of separation melt away. His hands splayed across her back, holding her like she was precious and necessary and his.

"Three weeks is too long," he murmured into her hair.

"Eighty-nine days left," she whispered back. They'd been counting down to Boston together like kids to Christmas.

"Get a room," Agnes said dryly, but when Kelsey pulled back, she caught the older woman hiding a smile. "After you eat this soup. And help with the banner. Liam made it too short."

Marcus kept one arm around Kelsey as he accepted the bowl with his free hand, the casual intimacy of it making her chest warm. This was new—this easy comfort, this assumption of closeness. Three months ago, they'd been stealing touches like criminals. Now, his thumb rubbed absent circles on her hip while he ate, and she leaned into his warmth without thought.

"What's the banner say?" he asked between spoonfuls.

"Nothing about ages," Cordelia said, going back to folding napkins. "Just 'Happy Day of Celebration for Our Favorite Person.'"

"That's... wordy."

"Katie's idea," all three sisters said in unison.

Kelsey laughed, feeling it bubble up from that place

that only existed here, with these people. "Where does it need to go?"

"Dining room," Agnes directed. "But you finish decorating that cake first. And Marcus, eat. You look like you haven't had a proper meal in days."

"Tuesday," he admitted. "Had a thirty-hour rotation that—" He stopped, shaking his head. "Doesn't matter. I'm here now."

His fingers found hers, sticky with frosting, and squeezed. She squeezed back, their private signal: *I'm here, we're okay, we're doing this together.*

"Right," she said, picking up the piping bag again. "One ring of garland, coming up."

"While I supervise," Marcus said, pressing a kiss to her temple before settling beside her. Close enough that their hips touched, far enough that she could work. The perfect distance, learned through months of practice.

Outside, snow continued to fall sideways as the wind whipped across the dune, but inside was warmth and sweetness and the particular magic of preparing to celebrate someone they all loved.

"Tell me about the MIT exhibition," Marcus said, stealing a fingerful of frosting.

She batted his hand away, but she was smiling. "Next month. They want to feature the lighthouse documentation project." She focused on a particularly tricky rosette. "Richard's coming to the opening."

"That's wonderful." His pride was genuine, warming her more than the kitchen's heat. "You'll be brilliant."

"We'll see." But she leaned into him slightly, drawing strength from his certainty. Three months ago, she would have deflected, hidden behind her camera, changed the subject. Now she let herself accept his faith in her work, in her talent, in their future.

"Five minutes to frosting that last layer," Beatrice announced, bustling past with what looked like her weight in butter. "Then we need all hands for the dining room transformation. Liam's already started on the photo displays."

"Photo displays?" Marcus asked.

"Mei-Lin at the inn, through the decades," Kelsey explained. "I've been digitizing the archives. You should see her in the sixties—she had this beehive hairdo that defied gravity."

"Don't let her hear you mention decades," Agnes warned. "She's been touchy about numbers all week."

Which was why they were throwing this party, Kelsey knew. Mei-Lin had been trying to let this birthday pass unacknowledged, still mourning David who'd always made productions of her birthdays. But the inn family had other ideas.

Kelsey's phone buzzed. She shot a hip his way. "Get that for me?"

Marcus pulled the phone out of her apron pocket, "accidentally" tickling her in the process.

"Surgeon's hands, he says," she said, but she was smiling.

Marcus checked the screen, and matched her smile. "Katie says they're at the tea shop. Mei-Lin's suspicious but distracted by the owner's latest acquisition—vintage Chinese teapots."

"Bless that girl," Beatrice said. "Though I don't know how she keeps coming up with distractions."

"She's got a list," Marcus said. "Color-coded by location and estimated time consumption."

"A Carter through and through," Agnes approved.

The frosting was done, the last rosette piped into place. Kelsey stepped back to admire her work—elegant scrollwork, tiny sugar peonies (Mei-Lin's favorite), and absolutely no numbers anywhere.

"Perfect," Marcus said, and she knew he meant more than the cake.

She turned to find him watching her with that soft expression that still made her stomach flip. Three months of long-distance hadn't dimmed it. If anything, the separations made these moments sharper, more precious.

"Dining room," Agnes commanded, breaking the spell. "Time to transform."

As they gathered supplies—banners and lights and

boxes of photographs—Kelsey caught Marcus's hand again. He pulled her close for a moment in the doorway, just the two of them in the space between kitchen warmth and dining room possibility.

"I love seeing you here," he said quietly. "Like you belong."

"I do belong," she said, surprising herself with the certainty. "Here. With you. With all of this."

His kiss was quick but thorough, tasting of soup and promise. "Eighty-nine days," he murmured against her lips.

"And counting," she agreed.

Then Agnes was calling for height and reach, Beatrice needed someone to carry the cake stand, and the afternoon blurred into preparation and laughter and the controlled chaos of a family preparing to show love through food and fuss and a lot of sugar.

The dining room transformation was already underway when they arrived, and Kelsey had to stop in the doorway just to take it in. Where this morning had shown the room in its everyday elegance—tall windows overlooking the lake, mahogany sideboard gleaming with careful polish—now it bloomed with decades of love made visible.

Liam stood on a short ladder, stringing lights around the window frames with the methodical precision of someone who'd been drafted into decoration duty before. The tiny white bulbs caught the late afternoon light filtering through glass, creating a constellation effect even before they were plugged in. His plaid flannel was dusty with whatever he'd been doing at the tool barn earlier, and there was a smudge of something on his jaw that Ella would probably fuss over later.

"Finally," he said without looking down. "Someone tall enough to help with the high corners."

"Nice to see you too," Marcus said, already shrugging out of his coat.

Only steps away from kitchen's sugar-sweet chaos, the dining room was its own olfactory world. Lemon oil on wood, the dusty scent of old photographs, fresh flowers—pink peonies and white roses that someone (probably Ella) had arranged in vintage crystal vases. But underneath lingered the permanent scent of the dining room: decades of shared meals, conversations over coffee, the particular mixture of contentment and tradition that seeped into the walls themselves.

"Where do you want me?" Kelsey asked.

"Photos," Ella said, emerging from behind the sideboard with an armload of frames. Her dark hair was twisted up with what looked like a paint stirrer, and there was glitter on her cheek. "We need to arrange them chronologically, but also aesthetically, but also so she sees the important ones first."

"So no pressure," Kelsey said, but she was already

moving to help, her photographer's eye automatically calculating spacing and sight lines.

The photographs told a story that made her chest tight. Mei-Lin through the decades—a teenager with hope in her eyes, working in the inn's kitchen while studying for her nursing boards. Meeting David at a town dance, their wedding in the parlor, building a life between two cultures. Later photos showed her with guests, always that particular combination of warmth and wisdom that made people trust her with their secrets.

"Oh," Kelsey breathed, holding up one particular photo. "Is this...?"

"Marcus, age five," Ella confirmed, grinning. "First summer at the inn. He's the one covered in mud."

Marcus groaned from his position holding lights while Liam attached them. "Why does that photo exist?"

"Because Aunt Mei-Lin documented everything," Kelsey said, studying the image. Five-year-old Marcus beamed at the camera, mud-splattered and gap-toothed, holding what appeared to be a frog. Behind him, Mei-Lin watched with fond exasperation. "Look how happy you were."

"I'd caught Frederick," Marcus said, as if that explained everything. "He was the biggest frog in the pond that summer."

"You named the frog?" Kelsey couldn't hide her delight.

"He named all the frogs," Liam interjected. "And the turtles. And three of the garden snakes. Drove Tom crazy."

The mention of Tom made everyone glance reflexively at the door. But Tom said he couldn't come; something "classified" had come up. But it could come down again, right? Liam said don't hold your breath; Ella said cross your fingers.

"This one goes in the center," Kelsey decided, holding up a photo of Mei-Lin and David from five years ago, before the cancer. They stood in this very room, surrounded by guests at some celebration, looking at each other like they were the only two people in the world. "She needs to see that we remember him too."

The dining room slowly transformed under their hands. Photos created a timeline along the walls, held by ribbons that Cordelia had somehow produced in exactly the right shade of dusty rose. The lights, once Liam and Marcus finished their complicated dance of ladder and electrical cords, cast everything in a warm glow that competed with the fading afternoon light.

"Table ready?" Agnes called from the doorway, surveying their progress with the critical eye of someone who'd overseen hundreds of events. "I've got the chrysanthemum plates and bowls, but I can't reach the box with the serving set."

"I've got it," Marcus said, but Kelsey caught his arm.

"We've got it," she corrected. Three months of partnership had taught them the value of shared tasks—and of stealing moments alone even in the midst of chaos.

The china closet was in the butler's pantry, a narrow space between dining room and kitchen that smelled of lavender sachets and silver polish. Marcus followed her in, and pulled the chain for the single bulb, casting shadows that made the small space feel even more intimate.

"Top shelf," Kelsey said, reaching, stretching failing. "I can see the boxes."

"Let me." He reached around her, pressing close in the narrow space. For a moment they just stood there, her back to his chest, breathing together. His free hand found her waist, steadying them both.

"I missed this," she said quietly. Not just the touching, though she'd missed that desperately. But this— working together, being part of something bigger than themselves, building traditions with their chosen family.

"June," he murmured into her hair. "June can't come fast enough."

She turned in his arms, the china forgotten for a moment. In the dim light, his face showed all the exhaustion that distance and residency had carved there.

But his eyes were warm, present, focused entirely on her.

"You're really here," she said, touching his face.

"I'm really here." He caught her hand, pressed a kiss to her palm. "For the whole weekend. No calls, no shifts, just us and this party and—"

"I love you," she said suddenly, the words escaping like they'd been building pressure all day. "I know we say it on calls, but I needed to say it here. Now. While you're real and solid and—"

"I love you too," he cut her off with a kiss. "Every day. Every minute. Even when you're just pixels on my phone screen."

"Especially then," she agreed, and then they were both laughing and kissing and nearly toppling the whole shelf of china.

They managed to extract the service set without breaking anything, though it was a close thing. By the time they emerged, the dining room had gained several more conspirators.

Mei-Lin's "special friend" from the tea shop in Traverse City had arrived, just happening to bring generous samples of the new blends from Yunnan. And the bookstore manager, Graham Cheever, who hadn't brought a gift but had loaned them a sound system that looked like it might blast them all out into the snow.

Everybody knew that Mei-Lin loved disco.

Graham was on a ladder now, adjusting speaker placement.

"No, it needs to angle toward the corner," Katie was saying, her blond hair crackling in the light as she gestured. "The acoustics—"

"The acoustics are fine," Graham interrupted, his jaw tight. "I've set up hundreds of—"

"Not in this room, you haven't. The ceiling height creates a—"

"Wait!" Ella said. "Katie, what are you doing here?"

"Helping Graham."

"No you're not," Graham muttered.

"I mean," Ella pressed on, "where is Mei-Lin?"

Katie shrugged, managing both to respond to Ella and slip her puffy coat off in the same move. "Yeah. Mei-Lin crisis. She wanted to come back early. Something about checking tomorrow's food delivery."

"Not the kitchen!" Beatrice bustled back to her domain.

"Stall her," Agnes commanded. "We need another hour minimum."

"How?" Katie demanded. "I've already taken her to every shop in town twice. I just dragged her down into the root cellar. What?"

All heads had turned to look at her.

"The... root cellar?" Marcus said.

"She said she wanted to look at food inventory. There's food there, right?"

"You did not lock her in the root cellar," Ella said.

"She's getting suspicious!"

"Like locking her in the basement's going to ease her mind," Graham said.

"Nobody asked you." Katie crossed her arms and glowered at him.

"Elder abuse," he whispered to her."

"Not listening," Katie said.

"Children." Agnes had one hand on a hip. Danger. Two hands meant flee the scene.

"I got it," Marcus said. "I'll tell her I need her advice on my car."

"Your car?" Katie looked bewildered.

"You know she's obsessed about safety." Marcus pursed his lips fake thoughtfully. "I think my Accord isn't working right."

"She won't fall for that," Katie said. "She knows you."

Marcus looked at Katie.

Who threw her hands in the air. "Walked right into that one, didn't I? Fine, I'll unjam the cellar—I did not lock her in, geez—and we'll try to figure out why my engine light keeps coming on."

"What!" Liam nearly dropped the folding ladder he

was carrying back to the closet. "Why didn't you say anything?"

Katie, guilt and glee mixed in her face, grabbed her coat and skipped out of the room.

Agnes nodded. "Half an hour, tops, that. We'll make do."

Shadows lengthened across the dining room's parquet floor as day headed toward evening. The Weimin porcelain gleamed on the crisp linen tablecloth that ran the whole length of the extendible wood table, each place setting a small work of art. Cordelia's napkin swans nestled beside water glasses that caught the light like promises. The photos on the walls told the stories of love and life, loss and choosing to love again.

"Music?" Ella asked, surveying their handiwork.

"Playlist ready," Graham confirmed

The front door banged open, making everyone jump. Katie's voice carried clearly: "—absolutely no idea how you did that! Thank goodness you were with me. I would have been completely helpless."

"A check engine light is hardly mysterious," Mei-Lin's voice replied, sounding deeply suspicious. "But those so-called car manuals are next to useless."

"You said it," Katie said, still too loud. "Oh, look, is that a new photograph in the hallway?"

Ella made frantic shooing motions. Everyone scattered to hiding positions with the practiced ease of people who'd ambushed loved ones before. Kelsey found herself tucked behind the sideboard with Marcus, his arm around her waist, both of them trying not to laugh.

"—really should check on tomorrow's menu," Mei-Lin was saying. "With so many guests arriving—"

"I'm sure Agnes has it handled," Katie's voice was getting closer. "Why don't we check the dining room first? I thought I saw... something."

"Something?"

"Something that needs... checking."

Even from their hiding spot, Kelsey could feel everyone's collective eye roll at Katie's improvisation skills.

The dining room door opened. For a moment, nothing—Mei-Lin must have stopped in the doorway, taking in the transformation. The lights, the flowers, the photos spanning a lifetime.

"What—" she began.

"SURPRISE!"

The shout came from every corner as people emerged from hiding. Mei-Lin's hand flew to her heart, her elegant composure cracking into genuine shock.

"You didn't," she breathed, eyes already filling as she took in the faces surrounding her—her inn family, her town friends, Marcus grinning beside Kelsey like he was seven again.

"Happy birthday," Ella said gently. "And before you

protest, we're not mentioning any numbers. Just celebrating you."

Mei-Lin moved into the room slowly, drawn to the photographs. Her fingers traced images—her young self, David through the years, Marcus muddy and grinning, countless guests whose lives she'd touched. At the photo of her and David, the tears started to flow.

She touched her chest again, taking in a breath.

"I believe I specifically said no fuss."

"When have we ever listened?" Agnes asked, producing a handkerchief from somewhere.

"Almost never," Mei-Lin admitted, accepting the cloth.

Marcus left Kelsey's side to embrace his aunt. Watching them together—the way she touched his face, the way he bent to accommodate her tiny frame—made Kelsey's heart expand. This was family. Messy and complicated and chosen and perfect.

And hers.

"Is that..." Mei-Lin had spotted something on the sideboard. A crystal vase filled with calla lilies. "Those are from Helena."

"Delivered an hour ago," Agnes confirmed. "With a card."

Mei-Lin extracted the small envelope with trembling fingers. Whatever the card said, it made her close her eyes and press it to her chest.

"Well," she said finally, voice steadier. "I suppose if you've gone to all this trouble, we should eat."

The cheer that went up could probably be heard at the lighthouse. People flowed toward seats, the careful choreography of a family that had shared hundreds of meals. Kelsey found herself between Marcus and Katie, and across from Graham and Agnes.

"Before we start," Ella said, standing at the head of the table, "I wanted to say something."

The room quieted, candlelight playing across faces warm with anticipation.

"Mei-Lin Chen Frankl, you taught me that love isn't just about finding the right person. It's about becoming the right person. It's about choosing to stay open even when loss makes you want to close. It's about believing in other people's love stories even when your own feels impossible."

She raised her glass, and everyone followed suit. "You've been the heart of this inn for longer than most of us have been alive. You've kept the magic alive, helped countless people find their way, and somehow managed to love all of us despite our many, many flaws."

"Speak for yourself," Katie interjected. "I'm flawless."

The laughter that followed was warm, familiar. But Ella wasn't done.

"So tonight, we celebrate you. Not for any particular number of years, but all of them. Every moment you've chosen love over fear, hope over cynicism, family over solitude. Thank you for showing us how it's done."

"To Mei-Lin," Marcus said, his voice rough with emotion.

"To Mei-Lin," the room echoed.

Mei-Lin was crying openly now, but smiling through it. "You terrible, wonderful people. You've ruined my mascara."

"Beatrice made three cakes," Cordelia offered. "That should help."

As laughter filled the room again and food began to appear—somehow multiplying beyond what anyone had prepared—Kelsey felt Marcus's hand find hers under the table. Their fingers interlaced with the ease of long practice, his thumb stroking patterns that made her skin hum.

"Look at her," he murmured, nodding toward his aunt, who was laughing at something Agnes had said, more animated than they'd seen her since David's death. "She needed this."

"We all did," Kelsey said, squeezing his hand. "These moments. This family."

"Eighty-nine days," he said quietly, but this time it didn't sound like longing. It sounded like promise. Like certainty. Like a future unfolding exactly as it should.

Katie overheard and smiled. "Have you found a place yet?"

"I've been looking," Marcus admitted. "There's a two-bedroom in Beacon Hill. Original hardwood floors, bay windows perfect for Kelsey's morning light obsession."

"It has exposed brick," Kelsey added, then blushed. "We've been touring places virtually. Together. On video calls."

"Very modern," Agnes approved. "In my day, you just showed up and hoped for the best."

"We want to see it in person next month," Marcus said, squeezing Kelsey's hand. "When I come for her MIT exhibition. Make sure it feels right."

Katie's eyes gleamed. "Apartment hunting. How domestic. What's next, joint bank accounts?"

The dinner progressed with the chaotic warmth of family gatherings everywhere. Multiple conversations overlapping, plates passed hand to hand, stories that everyone had heard but needed to hear again. The lights twinkled, the candles flickered. March's early darkness pressed against the windows, making the room feel like a ship of warmth sailing through winter.

"Speech!" someone called as Beatrice's cakes made their appearance—all three, because excess was love in the Thompson-Carter dictionary.

Mei-Lin stood slowly, one hand on Marcus's

shoulder for balance. The room quieted, even the old pipes seeming to pause their constant whispered conversations.

"I told myself I wouldn't cry anymore," she began, then laughed as tears spilled over again. "So much for that resolution."

She looked around the table, taking in each face. "When David died, I thought... I thought perhaps my chapter here was ending. That without him, I wouldn't know how to be in this place we loved together."

Her gaze went to Ella, with Liam beside her. "But you all wouldn't let me disappear. You kept pulling me back, kept reminding me that love doesn't end with loss. It transforms. It spreads. It finds new ways to bloom."

Her eagle eyes next caught Marcus and Kelsey's joined hands on the table. "You know, "David proposed to me on my birthday," she added, eyes twinkling as she looked up at Marcus. "Said he couldn't wait another day to start our life together. The best gifts come when you're ready to receive them, not when the calendar says it's time."

Marcus's hand tightened on Kelsey's. Message received.

Mei-Lin picked up her water glass, hand trembling slightly. "Thank you for not listening when I said no party. Thank you for knowing what I needed better than

I did. Thank you for being my family, my anchor, my reason to keep choosing joy."

"And thank you," she added with a watery smile, "for not putting however many candles on those cakes. My lungs aren't what they used to be."

The laughter that followed was mixed with tears. Until Graham fired up "Dancing Queen."

"Track One of my 'Mrs. Frankl's Dance Party' mix," he announced.

And then Agnes was directing the cake cutting with military precision, and the evening dissolved into sweetness and shared stories and the particular magic of a family celebrating one of their own.

Later, much later, Kelsey and Marcus found themselves on the inn's front porch. The snow had stopped, the wind had eased, leaving the world crystalline and hushed. Their breath clouded in the cold air, but neither suggested going inside.

"Good party," Marcus said, pulling her close against his side.

"The best," she agreed, fitting perfectly into the space beneath his arm. "Speaking of which, have you noticed the lighthouse has been on all evening?"

They both turned to look at the beam sweeping

steadily across the water, painting paths of light on the snow-covered beach.

"Hmm," Marcus said with studied innocence. "Strange. Liam must have forgotten to turn it off last time he was working on it."

"Right. Forgotten." She narrowed her eyes at him. "You've got that look."

"What look?"

"The one you get when you're planning something. The same one from December when you 'accidentally' needed help with the inn's Christmas decorations and somehow we ended up kissing under every single sprig of mistletoe."

"That was the inn's fault," he protested. "It kept moving the mistletoe."

"Uh-huh." But she was smiling, turning in his arms to face him fully. "What are you planning, Dr. Chen?"

"Right now?" he said softly. "I'm planning to kiss you on this porch where you first photographed me covered in snow."

"And then?"

"And then I'm planning to take you inside where it's warm and remind you that we have the whole weekend. No airports, no schedules, just us."

"And after that?"

His thumb stroked her cheekbone, eyes full of promises. "After that, I'm planning our life. Boston.

Lazy Sunday mornings. Fighting over closet space. Burning dinner because we got distracted. Normal, boring, perfect life things."

"That doesn't sound boring at all," she whispered.

"No," he agreed, leaning down to kiss her. "Not at all"

The kiss tasted like chocolate cake and promises and the aching sweetness of love that had survived distance and difficulty.

Behind them, the inn settled into nighttime quiet, satisfied with another successful match. The lighthouse continued its steady sweep, patient as always, waiting for whatever magic tomorrow might bring.

When they broke apart, Marcus kept her close, his forehead resting against hers.

"I need you to know something," he said, voice thick. "These three months, this distance—it's made me more sure, not less. Every time I drive here, every time I see you waiting..." He stopped, swallowed. "I used to think my mother was right. That eight days wasn't enough. But Kelsey, I'd know you in eight seconds. In any life. In any world."

Her breath caught. "Marcus—"

"You're it for me," he said simply. "My person. My home. My everything. And in eighty-nine days, I get to wake up every morning and choose you all over again."

She was crying now, not bothering to hide it. "You

can't just say things like that on a freezing porch when my mascara isn't waterproof."

"Sure I can," he said, thumbing away her tears. "I'm going to say things like that for the next fifty years. Better get waterproof mascara."

They stood there for a moment, just breathing each other in, the inn warm and glowing behind them, their future stretching ahead like the lighthouse beam across the water.

"Next year," Marcus said quietly, his arms tightening around her, "everything will be different."

"Different how?" She pulled back to look at him, catching something in his tone.

The lighthouse beam swept over them, illuminating his face fully. For a moment, she could see everything in his eyes—hope and certainty and something that made her breath catch.

"Just... different. Even better." He tucked a strand of hair behind her ear, the gesture so tender it made her heart skip. "We'll be living in the same city. Coming to family parties together. No more countdowns."

"No more goodbyes at airports," she agreed.

"And maybe..." He paused, his eyes holding promises he wasn't quite ready to voice. "Maybe some other new beginnings."

The lighthouse beam swept over them again,

bathing them in silver light, and Kelsey felt like the land itself was trying to tell her something.

Something just off the porch.

"What's that?" Kelsey pointed at a bunch of soft bootprints in the snow. They started at the edge of the short sidewalk to the porch, traveled the length of the house, and headed out to the dunes. "Snowshoes?"

Marcus leaned over the railing to get a closer look. "Two short, and fat. And with toes," he pointed them out.

"Not a deer, then?"

Marcus looked back at her, a mischievous look in his eyes. "A lynx."

"A what!" Weren't lynxes like tigers? Dangerous predators that shouldn't be anywhere near civilization?

"Relax. The only lynxes we have here are the stuffed kind that sleep on kids' beds."

"And the beds of some doctors, I'm told."

"Pure hearsay," Marcus said. "Must be kids. Or Katie. Keeping the town myths alive."

That's right. How could she forget that this was the town where you could find twenty different t-shirts that read "Green Arbor: Pawsitively Magical!" And buy any size Mama Lynx plushie.

She shivered. "What does Mama Lynx say, again?"

"Mama Lynx Says: Follow Your Heart!" Marcus sing-songed.

Exactly.

"Go inside?" he suggested. "Before we freeze to death and never make it to next year's party?"

"Mama Lynx says absolutely, yes."

As they came in from the cold, Kelsey caught a glimpse of the sand globe. The sand swirled gently, suggesting what looked like two figures standing at a lighthouse, but she didn't look closer. Some magic was better left mysterious.

For now, she had Marcus's hand in hers, a warm inn full of chosen family, and eighty-nine days until their another new chapter began.

It was more than enough.

It was everything.

Also by Annika Stone

Green Arbor Stories

Room for Magic

Room for Light

Room for Dreams

The Room for Magic Trilogy

Sweet Romance

The Author Next Door

A Taste of Tradition

Lilac Hearts

A Melody for Sunshine

Level Up to Love

Cosmic Hearts

Wild Hearts of Yellowstone

The Christmas Cookie Trap

Winter's Gift

The Valentine's Ruse

About the Author

Annika Stone is powered by caffeine and love. She doesn't have much time for writing. But someday...